CRESSIDA

Also by Clare Darcy:

Eugenia
Elyza
Regina
Lady Pamela
Georgina
Cecily
Lydia
Victoire
Allegra

CRESSIDA

by
Clare Darcy

WALKER AND COMPANY
New York

LS

First published in the United States of America in 1977 by the Walker Publishing Company, Inc.

Published simultaneously in Canada by Fitzhenry & Whiteside, Limited, Toronto.

ISBN: 0-8027-0575-8

Library of Congress Catalog Card Number: 77-73662

Printed in the United States of America

10 9 8 7 6 5 4 3 2 1

CHAPTER 1

The two occupants of the charming breakfast-parlour of
the house in Mount Street had each her head bent over
her correspondence on this fine morning in early May,
Miss Calverton dealing rapidly with the little heap of
cream-laid cards of invitation, letters, and household
bills that Harbage, the butler, had placed beside her
plate, and Lady Constance Havener brooding over a
single missive, very prettily written in a round, firm
hand, that appeared to have taken her attention to the
exclusion of the rest of her correspondence.

Miss Calverton, who was approaching her six-and-
twentieth birthday, looked, as she always did in the
morning before Moodle, her dresser, had had her in-
nings and transformed her into an elegant creature with
a deserved reputation in the *ton* for the highest degree of
dashing à la modality, rather like a schoolgirl, with her
tawny curls tied up with a ribbon and her lower lip
caught between her even white teeth in the concentration of her task. Lady Constance, who was four-and-fifty,
looked what she was—a handsome, slightly eccentric
lady of fashion whose ambitions to appear younger than

she was expressed themselves in an exuberantly modish negligee and a head of jet-black hair that was cropped behind and crimped wildly into curls in front, and whose statuesque form and uncompromising prominence of nose she attributed with pride to Plantagenet ancestry.

Her ancestry had not protected her, however, from what she was wont to term, in a voice of a dramatic colouring that might well have fitted it for the theatre, the slings and arrows of outrageous fortune, and, having been left, some half-dozen years before, a widow with a quite inadequate jointure by the late Mr. Jeremy Havener, who had had little to recommend himself as a husband beyond being the handsomest man in London of his time, she had been very glad to lend the somewhat erratic dignity of her presence to the orphaned Miss Calverton's household.

"I *do* think," she said now, still frowning over her letter as she broke the silence at last, "that people who wish one to do things for them ought not make one feel very wormlike for *not* doing them. Without saying a single word of reproach, that is. Or rather, I mean, without writing it, for after all this *is* a letter."

Miss Calverton, who was used to Lady Constance, glanced across the table at her briefly, quite unmoved by the darkly impressive manner in which this speech had been uttered, and, smiling in a way that enhanced the schoolgirl image, enquired who was making her feel like a worm.

"It is a girl I scarcely know," Lady Constance said. "Kitty Chenevix—my cousin Emily Mortmain's daughter. Emily married a Chenevix, you know, and they were horridly poor because he died almost at once and poor Emily was obliged to go and live in Devonshire. And now Kitty is nineteen and it is high time that someone brought her out, only her aunt Mills, who was to have done so, has been taken ill, and so she wonders if I might do it instead. All in the most *un*encroaching way, you see," she continued, glancing once more at the letter with a look of dissatisfaction upon her face, "merely hinting at the possibility in the most heart-rendingly timid manner, so that I shall feel the greatest beast in nature to refuse her—"

"Then why refuse her?" Miss Calverton asked practically, still with the greater part of her attention fastened upon her own letters.

"But, my dear Cressy—!"

Lady Constance became voluble. She hoped she knew better, she declared, than to invite any of her relations to stay in a house that was not her own, and, what was even worse, to foist a totally unknown young girl upon Cressida for an entire Season. There would be the nuisance of chaperoning her about to the Subscription Balls at Almack's, which were apt to be sadly flat for anyone who was not a debutante, a fond mama bent upon firing her daughter off into Society, or a gentleman interested in looking over the latest wares upon the Marriage Mart. And if the girl, by rare good fortune, turned out to be a belle instead of a Homely Joan for whom it would be quite impossible to find a husband, there would be young men plying the knocker at all hours of the day, and cluttering up the drawing room just when one most wished for peace and quiet.

"Not," Lady Constance, suddenly self-convicted of a lack of tact, hastened to add, "that *you* are not thoroughly accustomed to that upon your own account, my dearest Cressy, for I am sure the house is *besieged* by your admirers whenever you are in town—"

Cressida, who had been attending with only half an ear to her companion's protestations, at this point smiled mischievously and said in her crisp, warm voice, with its oddly offhand intonations, "Nonsense! Are *you* offering me Spanish coin, Lady Con? You know I am at my last prayers!"

Lady Constance bridled. "Well, I am sure there is

no need for you to be saying such a thing!" she observed tartly. "No one would take you for more than one-and-twenty if you did not make a point of telling them, and as for being at your last prayers—poh! *I* know you refused an offer no longer than two months ago from poor Gérard de Levalle—and *why* you must continue doing so," she added tragically, "I mean refusing offers from perfectly eligible men year after year, I cannot think. I am sure it never entered my head, when your great-aunt Estella died and I brought you to London for your first Season, that you would still be *Miss Calverton* half a dozen years later." She brightened suddenly. "But perhaps it will turn out to be all for the best in the end, with Langmere grown so *very* attentive since you have broken off with poor Gérard, for I cannot but think that it would be far more satisfactory to marry an English marquis than a French comte—*so* confusing with that monster Bonaparte going about creating all those extraordinary new titles, though of course *now* it is all quite as it was before the Revolution, with a Bourbon back at last upon the throne. But you really behaved quite shockingly to Gérard, you know," she continued, returning to her original grievance, "for I am sure you gave him every reason to expect that his suit would be successful—though not *quite* so badly as you did to poor Lord Mennin, crying off from your engagement to him *after* the notice had appeared in the *Morning Post*—"

Cressida looked rueful. She was not a Beauty in the accepted sense of the word, for, though she was fashionably tall and slim, she was not dark—the current mode— and her features were far from being cast in the classical mould. But there was something in that intensely alive face, with its hazel-green eyes and what one of her more poetical-minded admirers had called her *ripe-red, mocking, bitter-sweet mouth*, that made it quite apparent why she had never lacked for suitors since she had come to the notice of the *ton* six years before.

"Oh, dear!" she said. "You *do* make me sound a dreadful flirt, Lady Con! But I don't mean to be! Heaven knows, I had every intention of marrying Jack Mennin— only when it came to the sticking point—"

"You stuck!" Lady Constance finished it for her severely. "But you really *must* break yourself of that habit, my dear, before it becomes ingrained and you end up as an ape-leader—which is *never* an agreeable thing to be, no matter how extravagantly wealthy one is. It appears to me, in fact, that it might have been better for you if your great-aunt had *not* left you that huge fortune, for then you must have been obliged, like any genteel young female without expectations, to accept the first eligible offer that was made to you."

Cressida laughed. "Well, there is no use in thinking of that now, because she did leave it me," she said. "And if you are so bent on matchmaking this Season, Lady Con, I wish you *will* ask your young cousin to come to us; your energies in that direction will be far better expended on her behalf than on mine!"

She had finished with her letters now and took up the *Morning Post*, which lay beside her plate, and which, after a glance at what appeared to be a singularly dull budget of news upon foreign and domestic political matters, she turned to the page devoted to social intelligence. A notice of a *ton* engagement between the very plain middle-aged daughter of an earl and one of the many foreign fortune-hunters who seemed to have been loosed upon the town by the Peace elicited an amused comment from her, after which silence reigned until Lady Constance, who had gone back to pondering whether she really should accept Cressida's offer and invite Kitty Chenevix to Mount Street for the Season, was suddenly startled to hear an abrupt exclamation from her companion.

She looked enquiringly across the table. "What is it, my dear? Bad news?" she asked solicitously. "I do hope no one of our acquaintance is dead?"

"Dead? No! Resurrected, rather, I should say!" remarked Cressida, who appeared, now that Lady Constance observed her, to be suffering rather from a cool sense of distaste than from any grief of even the most minor nature. She flicked the open page of the journal before her. "It is only Dev Rossiter," she said. "He has returned from abroad and is visiting the Duke of York at Oatlands, with every intention, it seems, of coming up to town very shortly and 'doing' the Season. How highly respectable money *does* make one, to be sure!"

She folded the journal and put it aside rather sharply, while Lady Constance sat gazing at her with a rather puzzled expression upon her face.

"Rossiter?" she said after a moment. "I don't believe I—"

"Good heavens, Lady Con, of course you do!" Cressida said impatiently, without allowing her to finish her sentence. "He was one of the *on-dits* of the town last year. It was said, you know, that Rothschild, the financier, was the only man in England who knew the day after Waterloo that Wellington had not been defeated there, since he was actually in Brussels on the day of the battle and sailed across the Channel, as soon as he realised Bonaparte had been rompéd, to put his knowledge to good use here. He made a million pounds on 'Change by buying into the Funds at a time when everyone else was selling in a panic on the false intelligence that Bonaparte had already entered Brussels—but he was not the only man in England to accomplish such a *coup*. Rossiter duplicated the feat: he was in Brussels, too, on the day of Waterloo, and sailed across the Channel in an open boat in foul weather, only a few hours behind Rothschild, to make his own fortune by his dealings on 'Change. Surely you must have heard that gossip!"

"Of course I recollect, now that you have reminded me of it," Lady Constance said with dignity, "but you *know* I have no head for business, my love. The only thing that came into my mind when you spoke the name was that there was a gentleman named Rossiter whom your cousin Letitia mentioned to me once, who was in the Army and was most particular in his attentions to you while your great-aunt Estella was still alive, only of course an engagement was out of the question, as he was not at all a suitable person—"

"It is the same man," Cressida said. "And we *were* engaged—for all of a week. Then we had a blazing quarrel and broke it off—or perhaps I should say he broke it off."

"*He* broke it off?" Lady Constance looked scandalised. "But, my dear, no *gentleman* would—"

"Oh, Rossiter is a very odd sort of gentleman," Cressida said coolly. "By birth he has all the credentials—the younger son of a cadet branch of the Derbyshire Rossiters, one cousin an earl and another a bishop—but he had already been engaged in every imaginable sort of riot and rumpus even when I knew him, seven years ago. And though I understand he has not been in England since, except to carry out his Waterloo *coup*, there have been some very warm tales circulating about of his adventures on several continents, both in the Army and out of it."

"None," said Lady Constance, assuming an air of great propriety, "that *I* have ever heard, I am sure. It is my opinion, my dearest Cressy, that you encourage gentlemen to speak far too freely to you upon subjects that we females had much better know nothing whatever about. As for Mr. Rossiter, I am sure a Royal Duke may know whom he likes, but I do hope you will not feel obliged to renew *your* acquaintance with him when he comes to London. *Not* that I expect you would wish to, if he cried off from an engagement that I cannot help thinking you must have entered into only because you were a *very* young and inexperienced girl."

"You are quite right on both heads. I don't wish to, and I was—very young and inexperienced, that is," Cressida said, and went back to her *Morning Post.*

But when Lady Constance left the breakfast-parlour a few minutes later the *Morning Post* was laid aside again, and Cressida sat for some time with her chin in her cupped hands, frowning into space as her mind went back, almost in spite of herself, to the Cressy Calverton of seven years before.

Very young and inexperienced—that was an understatement, surely, for the girl who had been reared by a widowed mother, under circumstances of genteel poverty, in a village in the Cotswolds, and who had then, following her mother's death, lived for three years with an elderly, invalidish, and immensely rich great-aunt in Cheltenham. She had never in all her eighteen years met a man like Captain Deverell Rossiter when her uncle Arthur, descending upon her great-aunt Estella's secluded villa during race-week, had been moved—she could only suppose, by sympathy for her youth and the stifling atmosphere of lavender-water, hartshorn, and old age surrounding her—to carry her off to enjoy some of the social gaieties provided by Cheltenham in that midsummer season. He had taken her to the races and to the Assemblies, had bought her a new hat and a topaz set (Uncle Arthur, in spite of being perpetually out of funds, with Calverton Place sprouting new mortgages each year like spring flowers, was incurably generous), and, most important of all, had introduced Dev Rossiter to her.

That she should have fallen head-over-ears in love with Captain Rossiter within four-and-twenty hours of her first setting eyes on him was, she considered, in the light of her present half-dozen years' experience on the town, entirely predictable. She was young, full of restless energy and romantic fancies, and Rossiter, though certainly not handsome, had a kind of wary, sardonic charm that had already caused more than one impressionable female to overlook the more obvious disadvantages of his rather harsh-featured face and abrupt and quite unconciliating manner.

Why *he* had fallen in love with *her*—if he *had* fallen in love, instead of having been, as she now suspected, merely relieving what had undoubtedly been to him the tameness of a provincial race-meeting by a flirtation that had unexpectedly got into deeper waters—it was more difficult for her to decide. Certainly, she thought, Cressida Calverton, at eighteen, had had little to recommend her to an experienced and cynical soldier— neither conventional beauty nor manner nor fashion— but upon this point she was overmodest, for, though possessing none of these advantages, there had been a freshness, an eager reaching out for life by an unconventional mind and a vivid personality, that had caused a number of gentlemen to give more than a second glance during that race-week to the tall young girl on Arthur Calverton's arm, for all her obvious lack of town-bronze and her very dull though very good frock.

She herself, however, had had eyes for no one but Rossiter. He had asked her to stand up with him at the Assembly, asked her so negligently that she had been stung into a display of indifference quite foreign to her usual half-shy, half-eager manner. Then in the middle of the dance he had said to her abruptly, "What the deuce is the matter with you? If you didn't care to dance with me, why say you would?"—and they had been off. She had stiffened, had answered him with a frankness as unconventional as his own, and, quite regardless of the niceties of ballroom etiquette—with which, it had to be said in her defence, she had had little opportunity to become acquainted because of the secluded life she had led—had forthwith walked off the floor.

He had followed her. Within half an hour they had made up their quarrel and were talking to each other as if they had been acquainted all their lives; within four-and-twenty hours she had known she was in love with him; and within a week they were engaged. His regiment had been ordered to Portugal, but she was willing, even eager, to follow the drum with him. Of course great-aunt Estella had had to be informed; she had said little, but that little penetratingly to the point that they were both making utter fools of themselves, and had allowed matters to take their course.

Which of course they had, to the rapid denouement of one broken engagement and one (only one, Cressida was obliged to believe) temporarily broken heart. If Rossiter's own heart had suffered even the slightest crack, he had managed to conceal it very well both from her and from the rest of the world after that horrid evening when, as she had told Lady Constance, they had had a blazing quarrel and the engagement had been broken off.

Looking back at it afterwards, out of the miasma of bitterness and humiliation in which she had lived for the succeeding months, it had seemed to her that Rossiter had deliberately provoked that quarrel, for it had been he, she was sure, who had first suggested that she think twice before committing her future to the uncertainties of the career of an officer in a Line regiment in wartime. They were both, he had pointed out, without expecta-tions—for at that time no one had had the least notion where Great-aunt Estella intended to leave her fortune—and who was to blame her if she had leapt to the conclu-sion that his insistence upon this point meant that he himself had had second thoughts about the wisdom of marrying a portionless girl?

She had answered him, she remembered, disdainfully: his own temper was as rough and direct as hers was quick and impetuous, and words had been spoken that it was unlikely either of them would forgive or forget.

And so he had gone off to Portugal alone, and she, after a few months of a horrid kind of corrosive misery, as if acid had somehow got inside her and were eating away all the happy, eager expectations that, in spite of everything, she had always managed to keep bright there, had awakened one morning to find Great-aunt Estella dead and herself the possessor of a fortune beyond her wildest dreams.

It had often occurred to her since to wonder what Captain Deverell Rossiter had felt when he had learned that on the day he had broken off his engagement to young Miss Cressida Calverton he had thrown away a magnificent fortune as well. She would have been more than human if the thought of his chagrin had not spread balm over her misery—and more than human, too, if the change in her life brought about by Great-aunt Estella's death had not done much to erase the memory of that brief engagement from her mind. Lady Constance, a relation by marriage on her mother's side and a lady well acquainted in the fashionable world, had been hit upon by her uncle Arthur as the proper person to take her new household in charge and introduce her into the *ton*, and a hectic London Season had followed, in which offers of matrimony had been showered upon her like autumn leaves and she had, as Lady Constance had approvingly noted, "come on" amazingly in the social arts.

She had been engaged that first Season—engaged, it seemed to her now, more in order to prove to herself that, if Rossiter did not care to marry her, there were other men who did; but there had been none of that wildly magical happiness in the matter that there had been when she had been engaged to Rossiter, although the young man was handsome, the possessor of wealth and title, amiable, intelligent, and in every way the most eligible of *partis*. And in the end, she had cried off from the engagement, censuring herself as severely for doing so as the most conventional of dowagers might have done, but hiding her inner confusion under a coolness that had from that time forth gained her the reputation of being an accomplished and even heartless flirt.

Of course this reputation had not deterred a long list of gentlemen from seeking the rich and dashing Miss Calverton's hand in the years that followed, and more than one of them had carried the matter to the point that rumours of an approaching marriage had been circulated in the *ton;* but there had been no more engagements.

"Deuce take it," Cressida thought to herself with rueful severity, as she sat over the cold coffee-cups with her chin in hands, "I suppose I really *ought* to marry Leonard," who was Lord Langmere, the latest and most importunate of her suitors, a marquis, a power in the Government, a handsome man in his late thirties whose fortune equalled her own and whose tastes ran with hers towards politics, good conversation, and racing. "It is perfectly absurd to expect to feel again like a girl of eighteen loving a stranger *à corps perdu*"— and than Lady Constance put her head in at the door again and demanded in a despairing voice what she was to do about the Chenevix girl.

"Good heavens, ask her to come here for the Season, of course, if you have decided you care to go to the trouble of chaperoning her about," Cressida said, moved to this act of charity by her remembrance of another young girl who, until Great-aunt Estella had unexpectedly endowed her with a fortune, had been just as poor as Kitty Chenevix was, and reflecting as well that Lady Constance, who had much enjoyed managing the late Mr.

Jeremy Havener in his more manageable moods (which had occurred chiefly when there was no opportunity for him to wager money on anything), but had sensibly refrained from attempting to manage Cressida, who had a will of her own, would perhaps derive a good deal of satisfaction from manoeuvring Miss Chenevix into a suitable marriage.

Lady Constance looked gratified. "*So* generous of you, my dear!" she exclaimed. "And I expect she will really turn out not to be a great deal of trouble, after all, for she writes a very pretty, modest letter, and does not seem to be at all a *coming* sort of girl. I can just recollect seeing her at that little house Emily hired one year in Bath—she is quite a martyr to dyspepsia, you know: poor Emily, that is, of course, *not* the child—when she was only a little thing, very fair and quiet, I recall, and with charming manners. It would be *so* dreary to think of her never being given an opportunity to have even a single Season in town!"

Cressida agreed with proper civility that it would be very dreary, and, jumping up forthwith from the table, announced that she must go upstairs at once and dress, or she would be late for her appointment with Sir Octavius Mayr in the City.

"You know I *cannot* approve of your calling upon a gentleman at his place of business, my dear," Lady Constance said, for perhaps the dozenth time since she had taken up residence with Cressida. "It would be far more proper for him to wait upon you here"—but Cressida only laughed.

"Of course he would do so if I asked him to—and a great piece of impertinence it would be upon my part!" she said. "*Do* try to recollect, love, that Octavius is a man of vast importance in the City, and that the only reason he condescends to act as my man of business is out of a sense of gratitude to Great-aunt Estella. And if you tell me that he is not a gentleman," she went on, forestalling another of Lady Constance's familiar objections, "I shall remind you that Sir Walter Scott himself has spoken warmly of his wit and learning, that he has gathered what is considered to be one of the finest art collections in England, and that he has Royalty to dine at his house whenever he pleases!"

"Good heavens!" exclaimed Lady Constance in dismay, for, though she had heard this encomium before, it seemed to her it had never been delivered with quite so much spirit and feeling. "You are never thinking of marrying *him*, my love! He is *quite* old enough to be your father, by what I have heard, and, as fabulously rich and important as he may be, one cannot *really* call him—"

"A gentleman?" Cressida's mischievous smile was very much in evidence again. "Oh, no, something far better—the wisest man I know! But never fear—I am not at all the sort of female he would consider allying himself with, though I believe he *has* the intention to *ranger* himself with a lady of suitable rank and years when he is ready to retire from business. He discussed the whole matter with me very seriously one day, and I discovered myself weighed in the balance and found wanting—"

"Wanting! You! A Calverton!" exclaimed Lady Constance, in her deepest tones. "The man, my dear, is an impertinent fool!"

"Not at all!" said Cressida, laughing again, "though I won't say he is not riding his collector's hobbyhorse in this instance, with an eye out for obtaining only the rarest and most distinguished article of its kind. In fact, I have sometimes suspected him of having designs upon one of the Royal Princesses: there are so many of them, and all pining for husbands, poor things! But he was really quite complimentary in dismissing *my* pretensions. 'I see through you, my dear,' he told me, 'and yet I allow you to twist me around your little finger, which is a very poor situation for a husband to find himself in. What *you* need is a man who sees through you and can still stand up to all that will and charm—' "

"Well, that is Langmere. Langmere could do that," Lady Constance said stoutly, putting in a word for the absent marquis; but this statement was manifestly so absurd, since the love-stricken Lord Langmere would notoriously have gone through fire and through water, though much against his better judgement, at his beloved's bidding, that even Lady Constance felt she had not got the better of *that* exchange.

CHAPTER 2

Something less than an hour later Miss Calverton, stepping down from her carriage before a building near one of Wren's charming little City churches, St. Mildred's Poultry, was met by an obsequious clerk of Sir Octavius Mayr's and escorted upstairs to the elegantly furnished office where Sir Octavius himself was awaiting her.

"Well, Cressy?" he greeted her, with the lift of a quizzical eyebrow, as he rose from the large armchair in which he had been sitting behind a magnificent Bellangé desk decorated with green bronze paterae and resting on eight winged lions sculpted in mahogany. "Only a quarter hour late today? You are improving! Were you so late coming from the Campetts' ball last night that you could not bring yourself to leave your bed this morning, or am I to gather that the reason for your tardiness is that that fetching costume was donned for my benefit, and required a great deal of time and thought in the selection?"

Cressida, who was indeed looking very smart that morning in a walking-dress of water-green crape, with a daring hat à la Hussar set at a jaunty angle on her tawny curls, grimaced at him and regarded the Vulliamy timepiece that stood on the mantelshelf, its hands pointing uncompromisingly to three quarters past the hour.

"I daresay your clock is wrong," she said. "It can't possibly be so late."

"The clock," said Sir Octavius tranquilly, "keeps excellent time. I could wish, my dear Cressy, that one could say the same of you. However, in view of the charming picture you present, I am not disposed to cavil over a mere quarter hour."

He smiled at her—an amiably cynical smile that had made more people than Miss Cressida Calverton realise that there was very little use in trying the ordinary small social deceptions on him. He was a rather small, neatly built man, with a noble head crowned by iron-grey hair, and not a trace of his Danish origin lingered in his speech, despite the fact that he had been eighteen years of age when he had first come to England to begin his career there as a clerk in the offices of a well-known Baltic merchant.

Once there, his ascent in the world of business had been phenomenally rapid. Within the space of four years he had amassed a small fortune and set up in business for himself, at which time he had come to the notice of Miss Estella Calverton, who was then living in London. Miss Calverton, with her usual strong-minded eccentricity of behaviour, had taken him under her wing, introduced him into the literary and artistic *salons* she frequented, and entrusted her considerable fortune to his care—a course of action that had been amply justified over the years as that fortune had grown, under his management, into a truly splendid one.

Upon Miss Estella Calverton's death, Octavius Mayr (he was Sir Octavius by that time, having been knighted for services to the Crown not well known to the public, but of exceeding value to a monarchy perennially in financial distress over the French wars) had accepted the charge laid upon him in her will to act as one of her great-niece's trustees, the other being Arthur Calverton, who neither knew nor cared anything about finance except how mortgages and loans were arranged, and was quite content to leave the whole complicated matter of his niece's fortune in Sir Octavius's hands.

If Cressida had been an ordinary girl, there is little doubt that Sir Octavius would have managed, as soon as she had attained her majority, to shift his responsibility for her fortune on to other shoulders and go on about his own more important affairs. But Cressida was not an ordinary girl, and Sir Octavius, who had found the nineteen-year-old heiress shy, odd, and delightful, found her even more delightful, though no longer shy or odd, as her star had risen and attained its present shining eminence in the *ton*. He was not a man to whom it had ever been granted to fall in love, for finance was his golden and demanding mistress; but he sometimes congratulated himself upon the fact that he had not come upon Cressida twenty years earlier, when he might still have been young enough to have committed the folly of losing his head and his heart to a young woman who, however great her charm and however generous her spirit, he was well aware could be impetuous, self-willed, and, to the male mind, quite maddeningly unreasonable when she chose.

Having seen her comfortably ensconced now in a gondola armchair of gilded wood upholstered in green, he did not at once proceed to the matter of business he wished to discuss, but allowed himself instead the indulgence of a few minutes' social conversation with her. It had been several weeks since he had seen her, during which time the Regent's daughter, the Princess Charlotte, had been married with great ceremony to Prince Leopold of Coburg and the Byron scandal had come to a head with that disastrous ball at Almack's which had been given for him by his few remaining friends in the *ton* with the intention of rehabilitating him in the eyes of Society, but which had ended instead in abysmal failure.

"It was *horrid*," Cressida, who had been present, said in describing the affair to him. "The room simply emptied as soon as he walked into it. I do think he is a bit of a bore, with his posturings and the Cheltenham tragedies he is always enacting for one, but on the other hand I have not the least patience with Lady Byron. Any *sensible* woman would have known how to manage matters better than to land them both in the middle of all this scandal-broth. But from what I hear, she is enjoying her own martyrdom, and enjoying even more having made Byron a pariah to all England."

Sir Octavius said, with his usual cynical wisdom, that he dared say if the truth were known Byron was rather enjoying it, too, and would play Ishmael for all he was worth all over Europe, now that he had been driven out of England.

"And speaking of Ishmaels," he remarked, "I may tell you that you are about to be rewarded for your lack of punctuality by meeting the man who—though his reputation may not quite rival Byron's—will no doubt be taking his place this Season in providing the town with its more interesting *on-dits*. In other words, I am expecting the famous—or should I say, the notorious?—Captain Rossiter, and when he arrives I shall make a point of presenting him to you, so that you may boast to all your friends that *you* were the one who met him first."

He broke off, cocking an interrogative eyebrow at her, for in the not very agreeable surprise of hearing what he had just told her she had been unable to prevent herself from colouring up slightly and looking vexed. She herself was aware of this, and, with some annoyance at herself for such an unexpected piece of self-consciousness, managed to say in a cool and quite unconcerned voice, "Unnecessary! I am already acquainted with Captain Rossiter."

"Indeed?" Sir Octavius continued to look at her, the eyebrow still raised. "Do I detect, perhaps," he enquired after a moment, "a slight coolness in your tone?"

Cressida shrugged and said nothing.

"Yes," Sir Octavius answered his own question thoughtfully, "a very definite coolness, I believe! Now where, I wonder, can you have made the acquaintance of the dashing Captain? He has been so little in England, I understand—"

"It was in Gloucestershire, and years ago," Cressida said, preserving her indifferent air. "Do let us leave the subject, Octavius! If my being late to my appointment really has put you out, I wonder that you should wish to be wasting your time on gossip!"

Sir Octavius looked far from satisfied over this cavalier dismissal of the subject of Captain Rossiter; but he made no attempt to continue it, turning instead to the business he had to discuss with her. He had been agreeably surprised to find, upon first making her acquaintance, that she was quite capable of taking an intelligent interest in the management of her fortune, and he never made any important decision now concerning it without informing her fully. They accordingly had a brief and very businesslike conversation upon the matter of the latest investments he wished to make upon her account, and then there was a tap at the door and an elderly clerk, entering noiselessly, came in and murmured a few words in Sir Octavius's ear.

"Ah, yes! Show them in at once, Smollett," said Sir Octavius, with a glance at Cressida.

The clerk departed, and Cressida rose and began drawing on her gloves.

"I shall leave you to Captain Rossiter then, Octavius," she said. "I expect you will have a charming conversation—"

"What—running away?" Sir Octavius enquired, in mock-surprise. "It is not like you to be so poor-spirited, Cressy! What has Rossiter done to make himself so feared by you?"

"I am *not* afraid of Dev Rossiter!" said Cressida, with rather more emphasis than was strictly necessary. She stood looking indignantly at Sir Octavius for a moment and then sat down again. "Very well, I shall stay!" she said. "But only long enough to put the notion out of your head that I do not care to meet him. It is a matter of complete indifference to me!"

"Is it, indeed?" said Sir Octavius politely; and then, at the sound of footsteps approaching the door, turned his gaze in that direction.

The next moment a tall man in his middle thirties, with the black hair and disquietingly arrogant eyes of the dark Celt, and wearing riding dress instead of the more fashionable town costume of pantaloons and Hessians, appeared upon the threshold. He was followed by an equally tall, but somewhat younger, fair-haired man, with a modest manner and an agreeable smile.

Cressida, who had naturally been remembering a much younger Rossiter, had the peculiar sensation, as her eyes took in the dark face of the first arrival, with its harsh lines and direct, penetrating, rather cynical eyes, that she was looking at a stranger—one closely related, perhaps, to a person she had once known, but still a stranger. The shock of surprise was so great, in fact, that she scarcely heard his greeting to Sir Octavius and his introduction of his companion as Captain Miles Harries. Following these brief civilities, his eyes turned indifferently in her direction, and then paused there in a sudden hard, incredulous gaze.

As if that abrupt meeting of eyes had returned her presence of mind to her, she smiled at him composedly.

"Yes, it is really I," she said, in a voice that had suddenly become far more mannered than it had been when she had been talking to Sir Octavius, as if she were an actress who had just come on stage and had begun to speak her lines in the character of a dashing young lady of fashion. "How are you, Dev? Or perhaps I should say *Captain Rossiter?* It has been a very long time, after all, and our acquaintance was of a rather *brief* duration."

Rossiter did not return her smile. He was regarding her frowningly, still, it seemed, not quite believing what he saw.

"You've changed," he said abruptly, after a moment.

"But, my dear man, of course! One does, you know. After all, it has been years! Did you expect I should still be the same poor little green girl you knew in Cheltenham?" She turned to Captain Harries. "But we are being very uncivil! Won't you present your friend to me?"

Captain Harries was duly presented to Miss Calverton, and acknowledged the introduction with frank admiration and an accent that revealed itself at once, to Cressida's quick ear, as having no connexion with the higher ranks of English society. In spite of this, however, and of his being in company with the odious Rossiter, she liked him at first sight, for there was an engaging candour, mingled with a forthright kind of shrewdness, in his manner—a combination not often met with in fashionable circles.

"You are in the Army, then, Captain Harries?" she said, pointedly turning her attention to him to the exclusion of Rossiter, who, having sat down, was still subjecting her to a frowning scrutiny.

Captain Harries said he had been in the Light Bobs during the war, but had sold out when the Peace had come and was now engaged, in a small way, in Rossiter's present business ventures.

"Captain Rossiter, I may tell you," Sir Octavius put

in, addressing Cressida with a look of the blandest innocence upon his face, "not satisfied with his *coup* on 'Change at the time of Waterloo—of which I am sure you, along with all England, have heard—is now attempting to steal a march on the rest of us in the development of the new steam locomotives."

"Is he? But how too drearily respectable!" said Cressida, dismissing the subject with a cavalier lack of interest that made Sir Octavius long to shake her, and then wonder what even more drastic impulses were being repressed behind Rossiter's dark, impassive face. "And just when one was *so* depending upon you to run true to form," she continued, addressing Rossiter, "and enliven this very dull Season by doing something quite desperately *un*respectable! Like India—it *was* in India, wasn't it, that you ran off with the local potentate's favourite dancing-girl and very nearly caused a war?"

Rossiter's impassivity did not alter in the faintest degree. He turned civilly to Sir Octavius.

"We must make allowances for Miss Calverton, I believe, sir," he said coolly. "Most young ladies, I daresay, upon suddenly coming face to face with a man to whom they have once been engaged, experience an understandable shock to their tenderer sensibilities—"

Sir Octavius's right eyebrow, expressing intense interest, had risen at the phrase, *a man to whom they have once been engaged,* and Cressida's colour immediately heightened, but she managed to say quite composedly, "You may make yourself easy on that head, Captain Rossiter. I have no 'tender sensibilities' where you are concerned!"

"No, I daresay you haven't," Rossiter agreed, regarding her thoughtfully. "After all, when one has been engaged as often as you have, the matter no doubt becomes something of a commonplace. I believe I recall hearing that you were engaged to a viscount when I visited England briefly several years ago; now, if gossip is correct, we are shortly to felicitate you upon your betrothal to a marquis. May I enquire if it is your intention to stop at this point and actually marry this gentleman, or are you holding out for a duke?"

Even in the midst of her indignation at this really outrageous speech, Cressida found herself thinking swiftly that, if Rossiter found her changed, she could assuredly say the same of him. The Rossiter she had known in Gloucestershire would no doubt have given her quite as severe a set-down for her thinly veiled impertinences to him as the man who sat opposite her now had just done, but the words in that case would have been rough and direct, not couched in terms of a barbed and leisurely sarcasm even more telling than that which she had been able to turn upon him. Nor would he have faced her with this sardonic calm.

She said quickly and almost defensively, feeling herself at a disadvantage before the three pairs of masculine eyes regarding her with their various expressions of interested amusement (Sir Octavius), astonished discomfort (Captain Harries), and dispassionate expectation (Rossiter), "I am *not* betrothed to Lord Langmere! But if I ever should be, you may be assured that I shall certainly marry him!"

"Good!" said Rossiter, in negligent approval. "I am glad to see that in this case, at least, your intentions are honourable."

Cressida was about to say warmly that, considering that it was he who had made the first push to break *their* engagement, those words came rather oddly from him; she was forestalled, however, by his continuing at once, in the tone of one putting an end to a conversation of little importance, "But now, if you have no objection— my purpose in coming here was to discuss business matters with Sir Octavius, and I scarcely think we should be taking up any more of his time with trivialities."

This was such an obvious dismissal of her that Cressida at once resolved that, only to spite him, she would stay for another half hour, at least; and she would have done so, she assured herself as she took her leave, had it not been for the mortifying conviction that she had come off second best in this exchange. As she walked out of the room and down the stairs to her waiting carriage she remembered how often she had pictured, when she had first come to London and had shed her greenness like a butterfly shedding its cocoon, how she would behave when she next met Captain Deverell Rossiter, in a London ballroom, or at the theatre, or while she was riding in the Park. How coolly self-assured she had always been in those mental encounters, and how utterly she had crushed any pretensions upon his part to a resumption of their former degree of intimacy!

Yet now, when almost seven years had gone by, when she was the petted darling of the *ton*, a lead in fashion acknowledged by all, she had allowed herself to be betrayed into losing her temper like a schoolgirl, while he had clearly demonstrated, not only to her but to Sir Octavius and Captain Harries as well, that he was so far from wishing to put himself upon terms even of the most ordinary friendship with her that he had not the slightest compunction in being abominably rude to her. "When one has been engaged as often as you have, the matter no doubt becomes something of a commonplace," he had dared to say to her, and she vowed to herself that if it was the last thing she did in her life she would marry the Marquis of Langmere in a very public and exceedingly fashionable manner in St. George's, Hanover Square, with the entire world of the *ton*, plus Captain Deverell Rossiter, looking on.

And then, having got into her carriage in a fine rage and directed her coachman to drive to Bruton Street, where one could always purchase a frivolous and shockingly expensive new bonnet calculated to make the bones of any even moderately susceptible member of the male sex turn to water when he saw it set upon a crown of tawny curls and shading a pair of the most brilliantly sparkling eyes in all England, the humour of the situation overcame her and she began to laugh. They had certainly, she and Rossiter, treated Sir Octavius and Captain Harries to a brief but spirited battle-royal that it seemed to her—though she had not, of course, been present upon that celebrated occasion—might cast the contest between Molyneux, the Black, and Champion Tom Cribb in the shade.

"They will be laying bets at White's as to which of us will come out the winner if we are not careful!" she told herself. "Poor Captain Harries! I wonder what on earth he must think of me! But let me hope for the best. Perhaps, if luck is with me, I shan't be obliged to meet Rossiter again."

But she still went on to Bruton Street, all the same, to buy that shockingly expensive and fatally attractive bonnet.

CHAPTER 3

Lady Constance, meanwhile, had sent off her invitation to Miss Kitty Chenevix to spend the Season in Mount Street, and some few days later was rewarded by a letter despatched by that young lady by return post, announcing her imminent arrival, and thanking both Lady Constance and Miss Calverton in the warmest terms for their kindness. Lady Constance, of course, showed the letter to Cressida, who agreed that Miss Chenevix had expressed herself just as she ought, and that she would no doubt be found to be a very pretty-behaved girl, whom it would be quite agreeable to have in the house.

It was true that by this time Cressida had had some slight misgivings as to the wisdom of having invited into her home for an extended period a young girl who might, for all she knew, turn out to be either an unmanageable hoyden or a dead bore; but the arrival of Miss Chenevix herself a few days later put a decisive period to these troublesome speculations. Cressida, entering the front door one morning after a ride in the Park with Lord Langmere, found herself face to face with a slight, fair, very attractive young girl in an earth-coloured travelling dress and a chip hat, who was being greeted by Lady Constance while Harbage supervised the removal of her modest portmanteau and a pair of bandboxes to an upper floor.

"Oh, Cressy, my dear! Here is Kitty," Lady Constance said at once, drawing Miss Chenevix forward towards Cressida. "And this is Miss Calverton, my love. Only think, Cressy," she continued immediately, forestalling Kitty's attempt to speak, "she spent the night in a horrid little inn in Turnham Green only because she did not wish to put us out by arriving so late in the evening! Was not that thoughtful of her? But really quite unnecessary, as I have just been telling her—"

"Yes, quite," Cressida said pleasantly. "But do come into the morning-room and sit down, Miss Chenevix—or shall I do away with formality and call you Kitty at once?"

She was accustomed to making up her mind very quickly about the people she met, and she immediately decided, as Kitty smiled at her a trifle timidly and said, "Yes, please do!" that neither she nor Lady Constance need have any qualms over their invitation to Miss Chenevix. There was something very taking in her manner— a kind of quiet, modest self-composure with only the slightest hint of an appealing timidity; and her appearance was entirely prepossessing. She had a slender, elegant figure and a delicately boned face, somewhat over-thoughtful, it seemed, for her years; her hair, very fair, almost flaxen, was arranged simply, in a becomingly girlish fashion, and her blue eyes were set wide apart under softly pencilled brows.

All in all, Cressida thought approvingly, as she sat down opposite her in the yellow morning-room, an entirely presentable young girl—not a diamond of the first water, certainly, but all the same she might do very well for herself in London, even with her deplorable lack of fortune, under the aegis of Miss Cressida Calverton and Lady Constance Havener.

As for Miss Chenevix herself, her first concern, when she found herself seated in the morning-room with Cressida and Lady Constance, was to express her gratitude to them for agreeing to sponsor her come-out in London.

"I am afraid you must have thought me dreadfully forward to write to you," she said in her soft, clear voice, turning to Lady Constance. "But Mama has always spoken so much of you that I feel as if I know you a great deal better than I do, and I did not quite realise that— that I should be imposing upon Miss Calverton as well—"

"Nonsense!" said Cressida. "There is no question of 'imposing.' Lady Con and I will enjoy the Season a good deal more with someone with us to whom everything is new. I do hope you are prepared to like parties and balls? A friend of mine, Lady Dalingridge, is giving one tomorrow night, and she asked me to bring you with me when she learned you were to be my guest. It will be a dreadful squeeze, I expect—her parties always are—but you will meet everyone who is anyone, and I shall introduce you to every eligible young man I can manage to lay my hands on."

Kitty, her face flushing up with pleasure, said she would enjoy it of all things.

"Then we must have a look at once at your wardrobe," Cressida said practically, "and see what you are to wear, for nothing is more important than the first impression one makes." She paused, seeing that the flush, no longer, it seemed, one of pleasure, had suddenly mounted higher in Kitty's face. "Never mind; you need not tell me!" she said briskly. "You have nothing that is not ever so slightly dowdy, or not quite in the mode, or suitable more for a provincial assembly than a London ballroom—is that it? I know all about that—I was not always so well to pass, you know!" Her eyes ran quickly over Kitty's slender figure. "We are almost of a height, I think," she said, "though you are perhaps a shade the slenderer. Moodle—my dresser—will take care of that. She is very clever with her needle, and though it would not do for you to appear in your first Season in most of my gowns, I am sure I shall be able to find one or two that will raise no eyebrows if you wear them. Come along; we shall go upstairs and see."

She rose, and Kitty, looking a little dazed by this masterful intromission into her affairs, followed her upstairs to her bedchamber, where Cressida at once began pulling dresses out of the tall French garderobe.

"But I couldn't—Miss Calverton, I really *can't*—" Kitty protested, her blue eyes lighting up with incredulous pleasure, nonetheless, like any other young girl's, at sight of the exquisite creations Cressida was tossing on to the bed for her inspection. "Mama gave me a fifty-pound note before I left," she continued, in the tone of one announcing the possession of untold riches, "and she said if I needed anything I must use it to buy it—"

"Fifty pounds!" Cressida said, smiling. "Yes, that will do very well when you have a desire to see the Pantheon Bazaar, and discover a pair of silk stockings, or a smart sunshade, that you find you really cannot do without. But gowns are quite another matter. They are horridly expensive, and if I were to send you to Fanchon she would gobble up that entire fifty-pound note, and more, only to provide you with one moderately tonnish carriage dress. As for evening frocks—they are quite out of the question!" She held up a gown of white spider-gauze embroidered with silver acorns, its demure bodice fastened down the front with tiny satin rosettes. "This will do, I expect," she said. "I can't think what made me buy it, for I am certainly past the *ingenue* stage—but you will agree that it is very pretty! It should become you admirably. Do try it on, and if it should require alteration, Moodle will be able to attend to it before tomorrow evening."

There was nothing for it but for Kitty to don the frock, and in a few minutes she stood gazing at herself in the glass, her protests quite stilled by what she saw there, while Cressida rummaged in drawers for the elbow-length French kid gloves and the silver net drapery that she said would be necessary to complete her young protégée's costume.

Lady Constance, coming upstairs a few minutes later to tell Cressida that she really must change out of her riding-dress so that they could pay morning-calls upon the Duchess of Webwood and Lady Camlin, who had just arrived in town, found Moodle down on her knees beside Kitty with her mouth full of pins, which did not prevent her from carrying on a spirited though somewhat unintelligible dispute with her mistress on the desirability of Cressida's presenting to Kitty a gown of pale primrose sarsnet. White, she said, or, at the most, pale pink or blue, was far more suitable for a young lady in her first Season.

"Oh, Lady Constance," said Kitty, turning upon her a face which, even while glowing with excitement and pleasure, still managed to maintain its air of quiet composure, so unusual in a girl of her age, "you cannot think how kind Miss Calverton has been to me! She has given me this gown, and an opera cloak, and so many other things that I am sure I must be grateful to her all my life!"

Cressida laughed and said that wouldn't be necessary; Kitty need only enjoy herself at the ball on the following evening and she would be quite sufficiently repaid. Half an hour later, when she and Lady Constance were in the carriage on the way to pay their morning-calls, Lady Constance said in a judicial voice that, really, it might be far less fatiguing than she had imagined to chaperon Kitty about, so very pretty as she was, particularly with Cressida seeing to it that she would appear to the greatest advantage wherever she went.

"I daresay I shall be able to arrange quite a respectable match for her," she said, "which was scarcely to be hoped for, I fear, if she had gone to her aunt Mills, who does not, I believe—though I am not acquainted with her myself—move in the first circles. Indeed, it turns out to be very fortunate for Kitty that Mrs. Mills *was* taken ill, though no doubt it appeared a great tragedy to the child when she first heard she was to be disappointed in her hope of coming to her this Season."

Cressida agreed, and the subject of Kitty was forgotten until, upon returning to Mount Street, they enquired after her and were informed by Moodle that she was upstairs in her bedchamber, mending a rent that Moodle had discovered in the flounce of one of Cressida's evening frocks.

"Really, miss, she quite begged to do it," said Moodle, when Cressida expressed a good deal of disapproval and surprise over Kitty's having been set to such a task, "and I must say she is as clever with her needle as any seamstress, and is setting such tiny stitches as you wouldn't believe. A very pretty-behaved young lady, miss, if I may say so, and with such an elegant complexion and figure, it will be a real pleasure to dress her, I'm sure!"

These words of approval from the austere Moodle, who had had her nose in the air over the notion of a young lady arriving as a guest in the house without her own maid ever since Miss Chenevix's visit had been announced, caused Cressida and Lady Constance to exchange glances.

"A paragon, in fact!" Cressida commented, as they went up the stairs together. "If she has got round Moodle, I shall not put even a marquis past her skill!

Had I best hide Langmere from her, do you think?"

Lady Constance, who was rather literal-minded, said seriously that she did not quite think that would be possible, as he was so often in the house that Kitty must be sure to meet him; but added that his lordship was obviously so much in love that it appeared highly unlikely he would be attracted by another female, particularly one so young and unformed as Kitty.

"Yes, but one never knows about gentlemen," Cressida said, unable to resist the temptation of continuing the jest. "Langmere is well past thirty, and has never married; there have been more cases than one of men of that age who have made cakes of themselves over schoolroom misses, you know!"

Lady Constance looked with some consternation into her face, but, seeing Cressida's primmed-up lips and dancing eyes, her anxiety relaxed.

"Now you are funning again, my dear!" she said severely. "But, really, it is *not* a matter for levity. Langmere is quite the most agreeable man in London, to say nothing of his being by far the most eligible, and fond though I am prepared to be of Kitty, I cannot think it would be at all proper for her to steal him from you. *Not* that I am persuaded she could do so, but—"

"But there is no relying upon gentlemen. Indeed, no!" Cressida finished it for her, with a mischievous glance. "They are kittle-cattle creatures, are they not? Always running after the latest sensation! And yet they have the temerity to say it is *we* who are fickle!"

They found the subject of their discussion, as Moodle had informed them, in her bedchamber, carefully putting the last exquisite stitch into the torn flounce of a gown of pomona-green sarsnet.

"But you really must not do such things for me!" Cressida protested. "You are here to enjoy yourself—and it is *quite* unnecessary!"

And the next moment she wished she had not spoken, for Kitty, looking hurt, said really, she had loved doing it because Miss Calverton had been so very kind to her—after which Cressida, self-convicted of base ingratitude, felt obliged to fall back upon admiring her needlework and averring that she was quite sure Moodle herself coud not have done it so well. It would be a trifle wearing, Cressida thought, as she escaped a few minutes later to her own bedchamber, if Kitty was going to be so very grateful to her that she herself would constantly be obliged to be grateful in return. But she consoled herself with the thought that, once young Miss Chenevix found herself immersed in the ceaseless round of balls, Venetian breakfasts, theatre-parties, and routs that would be offered for her diversion during the London Season, she would lose some of this excessive zeal to show herself properly appreciative of what was being done for her.

And, indeed, when the following evening arrived and Cressida came downstairs to the drawing room, where Lady Constance and Kitty were already seated, awaiting the arrival of Lord Langmere, who was to escort them to the ball, she found her young protégée as full of absorbed excitement as she could have wished. Cressida, casting a critical eye over her, was inclined to agree with Lady Constance's satisfied observation that she was sure to be a success. The gown of white spidergauze gave her the fragile appearance of a fairy princess; her very fair hair had been dressed by Moodle's skilful fingers in an aureole of curls that softened the slight angularity of her delicate features; and her toilette, thanks to Cressida's generosity, was complete to the last fashionable detail of white satin sandals, long kid gloves, and the length of silver net drapery caught up over her arms at the elbows.

If Lady Constance still harboured any slight apprehension that Kitty's youthful charms would cause Lord

Langmere to swerve for a moment from his devotion to Cressida, however, she was soon made to realise that her fears had been groundless. Lord Langmere, who was a pattern of courtesy, did indeed acknowledge his introduction to Miss Chenevix with every appearance of polite attention, but it was obvious that his eyes were all for Cressida, who herself appeared to great advantage that evening in one of Fanchon's most fashionable creations—a gown of jonquil Italian crape, deeply décolleté, with the scalloped flounce that finished its hem revealing rather more of a pair of slender ankles than a less dashing young lady would have deemed quite proper.

Lord Langmere, however, though the soul of propriety himself, showed no sign of disapproval, and on the contrary complimented her appreciatively upon her appearance. He was a handsome man in his middle thirties, vigorous and virile, with a well-set-up figure admirably suited to the evening fashion of severely cut, form-fitting coats, knee breeches, and silk stockings, and, like any gentleman of the *haut ton*, would have been disappointed in the gown worn by the lady of his choice only if it had not conformed to the latest and more daring whim of the current mode.

As he seated himself in his elegant town-chariot, having first seen his three ladies comfortably settled on its velvet cushions, he said to Cressida with the attractive, rather indolent smile that had fluttered more than one feminine heart and caused even his most acerbic political opponents to admit that he was an excellent sort of fellow, after all, "Dolly is not to disappoint us tonight, I understand. You know her boast that she has never yet failed to present her guests with the unusual at her parties? Well, she has got Rossiter tonight. Had she told you?" As Cressida, in whom several odd and, on the whole, disagreeable sensations had been aroused by this announcement, did not immediately reply, he went on,

"You *do* know who he is, of course? The man who out-Rothschilded Rothschild and crossed the Channel in an open boat in impossible weather after Waterloo to carry out a dazzling *coup* on Change? He has at last returned to England now; York had him at Oatlands for a few days, but he has been too much occupied with his own affairs, it appears, to accept any other invitations until tonight. It is like Dolly's luck to nobble him first."

Cressida said a trifle crossly that she did not consider Dev Rossiter such a prize acquisition that Dolly Dalingridge needed to boast about it.

"Oh," said Lord Langmere, looking surprised. "Are you acquainted with him, then?"

"I am not only acquainted with him, I was once engaged to him," Cressida said with some asperity, "as he has no doubt been going up and down London telling everyone who will listen to him this past week. He certainly lost no time in reminding *me* of it very publicly in Octavius Mayr's office, when I had the misfortune to run across him there."

Lord Langmere, appearing somewhat daunted, said, "Oh," again, for want of being able to think of anything better to say, which moved Lady Constance to leap into the breach and inform him kindly that it had all been ages ago, before Cressida had ever come up to London, and had lasted only for a week.

"All the same," Lord Langmere, who had by this time somewhat recovered himself, said firmly, "it appears to me that he should certainly not have spoken of it to Cressy. A bit of a coxcomb, I gather? Well, I daresay one should have expected it—all these really very odd stories going round about his adventures abroad—"

"He is *not* a coxcomb," Cressida said indignantly. "I may have been excessively green when I lived in Cheltenham and became engaged to him, but I have never been so idiotish as to form an attachment for a coxcomb!

He is only insufferably rude, and *quite* selfish, and I can't see why all this fuss is being made over him! And," she added dangerously, "if anyone else tells me about his sailing across the Channel in an open boat in impossible weather, they will soon discover how insufferably rude *I* can be!"

Lord Langmere looked slightly apprehensive, and not without reason, for the first words Cressida heard from Lady Dalingridge's lips, when she trod up the crowded staircase of Dalingridge House a few minutes later to be greeted by her host and hostess, were, "Oh, Cressy, my dear, have you heard? I have Rossiter coming tonight! Yes, actually! He is the man, you know, who crossed the Channel in an open boat—"

CHAPTER 4

It was impossible, of course, for a young lady of fashion, standing under the blaze of a crystal chandelier at the head of a grand, red-carpeted staircase thronged with dozens of the most illustrious members of London Society, all chattering briskly in an aura of silk gowns, superbly cut evening coats, expensive perfumes, and impressive orders as they awaited their turn to be announced to their host and hostess, to be insufferably rude to anyone; and if she had been, no one would have noticed.

Lady Dalingridge certainly would not have done, being extremely shortsighted and having momentarily let her *face-a-main* fall as she imprudently took both of Cressida's hands in hers. Nor would Lord Dalingridge, who disliked balls and had cultivated, over the quarter-century during which his marriage to an extremely gregarious wife had obliged him to endure them, a habit of not listening to anyone and confining his own conversation to an occasional interrogative grunt or hasty, "Yes, indeed!" while he mentally replayed the more interesting hands of the whist game he had enjoyed that day at Brooks's.

[41]

Cressida, who was quite aware of all this, seethed, therefore, in secret, but in public performed her duty of making Kitty known to Lord and Lady Dalingridge, and it was not until she had seen her young protégée safely partnered with Lord Langmere, and joining the set just then forming in the ballroom for a country dance, that the opportunity was presented to her to express her opinion upon the attention that was being lavished on Rossiter by the more sensation-hungry members of the *haut ton*.

And even then she did not do it properly, because the opportunity came in the person of the Honourable Drew Addison, who enjoyed the reputation of possessing —always excepting Mr. Brummell, of course—the sharpest tongue and the most blighting eyebrow in London. He had never, however, quite been able to challenge Brummell's position of *premier dandy*, the general opinion being that, while his tailors, inspired by his acerbic demands, provided him with coats of the most exquisite fit, and while his neckcloths expressed the purest of tastes combined with an almost fiendish skill in arrangement, there was a certain rigidity in the man himself that prevented him from attaining the negligent ease of manner so essential to becoming the prince of fashion that Brummell was.

Addison was a man in his late thirties, tall and handsome, if one was prepared to overlook a rather large nose and the iciness of the blue eyes under those supercilious brows. Cressida disliked him, but admitted him to her inner circle because he was amusing and extremely difficult to exclude from any gathering—"like a wasp at a picnic," she had once said of him, which remark, having been repeated for his benefit by a helpful friend, had not endeared her to him, and had resulted in the circulation of several rather disagreeable aphorisms concerning her throughout the *ton*, which had in turn been repeated to her and to which she had paid no attention at all.

He had been standing at the other side of the crowded ballroom when she had come in, but, as he always took pains to be seen in conversation with every person of consequence during the course of a social evening, he at once deserted the very minor European Royalty to whom he had been speaking and came across to her.

"Such unrewarding young bores, these German princelings we have had swarming to England ever since Leopold carried off our young Princess," he remarked to her, looking down his nose at his erstwhile companion, after the initial civilities had been exchanged. "Like prize cattle—very fat, very dull, and with smallish, obstinate eyes. And most of them, I daresay, without a penny to bless themselves with, so that if you should be cherishing a secret desire to become a *Prinzessin*, dearest Cressy, I am sure you have only to throw your handkerchief and there will be a positive scramble to pick it up. Did you know that when Leopold himself first visited London two years ago he could not afford to stop at an hotel and set himself up instead in lodgings over a grocer's shop in Marylebone High Street? That, of course, was before the Princess Charlotte took him up. The advantages to a young man of having fair hair, hazel eyes, a well-set-up figure, and engaging if somewhat priggish manners, cannot, it seems, be exaggerated in this modern age."

Cressida said he and the Princess appeared to be very happy, and that she dared say the Princess did not regret now having broken off her engagement to the Prince of Orange, in spite of the furor it had caused at the time. She then bit her lip, wishing she could take back her last remark, as it obviously presented Addison with a perfect opportunity to speak of another broken engagement, namely, hers to Rossiter.

But, somewhat to her surprise, the subject was not brought up, and she was obliged to believe, with a slight sense of chagrin, that she had misjudged Rossiter in accusing him of spreading the tale of that old engagement about, for if anyone else in London, beyond the four persons who had been in Sir Octavius's office that morning, had heard of it, it was certain that Addison would have done so as well. He knew everyone's secrets, and had no scruples about using them to their owners' discomfort.

It was too much, however, to expect that Rossiter's name would not be brought up at all, which it promptly was, Addison observing in his usual bored way that the lion of the evening, it appeared, had not yet arrived, preferring, like all lions, to do his roaring before the largest possible audience.

"And how many woolly lambs," he went on, casting a jaundiced eye over the brilliant room, "in the shape of marriageable young ladies with ambitious mamas, are to be trotted out this evening for his inspection, I leave it for you, my dear Cressy, to determine. A half-dozen fabulous Indian rubies—I daresay you have heard that that was the source of the money he plunged with on 'Change?—transformed into a solid English fortune, will wash out any number of 'damned spots' in a man's past, it seems, in spite of anything Lady Macbeth may say. To continue in the Shakespearean vein, I could a tale unfold, my love, on the subject of Captain Deverell Rossiter, whose lightest word would harrow up thy soul, freeze thy young blood—"

"Do stop declaiming, Drew!" said Cressida. "Next you will be telling me that you will cause my knotted and combined locks to part and each particular hair to stand on end, like quills upon the fretful porpentine—which is not at all in the mode, you know. And I daresay half the stories that are being told of Captain Rossiter are not true, at any rate. Dolly is quite capable of inventing half a dozen hair's-breadth escapes and amorous adventures singlehanded, only to make her party more interesting."

"But I do *so* agree, my dearest love," said Addison. "Undoubtedly he will turn out to be an entirely tame lion, and quite dreadfully dull, as most men of action are. By the bye, I daresay he *is* a gentleman? I have just had the misfortune to be presented to a Captain Harries, who appears to be not only a business associate of his but a close friend as well, and I can assure you that *he* is not *quite* the thing."

"Captain Harries? Is he here?" Cressida looked quickly about the room, and had no difficulty in discovering the object of her search at its other end, for as the Captain was head and shoulders taller than most of the other guests, his fair head emerged like the dome of St. Paul's from the lesser edifices surrounding it. "I must go and speak to him," she said. "I am quite sure he doesn't know a soul in this room, and in spite of your slighting remarks, Drew, he is really a very agreeable person."

"My dear Cressy, to win such a charitable statement from *you*, he must be a paragon! But pray don't go yet. I want you to present me to your young protégée when Langmere has finished his duty-dance with her. A Miss Chenevix, I understand? A relation of Lady Con's?"

"Why be interrogative, my dear, when you already know all about it?" asked Cressida, not at all surprised to find Addison wishing to be beforehand of everyone else in the room in discovering all there was to be discovered about Kitty. "But I shall be delighted to present you to her," she went on, "if you will promise me to do your possible to bring her into fashion. She is Barry Chenevix's daughter, you know, and I need not tell you there is no fortune there, so Lady Con will be grateful for help from any quarter in firing her off this Season."

"If she has *my* help, dear Cressy, she will need no other," said Addison, who had never been known to hide his light under a bushel. He raised his quizzing-glass the better to survey Kitty as she moved with lightness and precision in the dance, the natural delicacy of her slight figure enhanced by the shimmering white spider-gauze gown. "Passable," he remarked presently, letting the glass fall,"but not likely to cause a stir. You will be fortunate to get her off this Season in spite of that gown, in which I certainly detect Fanchon's hand—"

"Luckily, everyone is not so particular as you are," Cressida said, shrugging slightly. "I fancy she will do well enough: she has the knack of making herself agreeable. Will *you* be agreeable enough to stand up with her for the next set? You know how her credit will rise if it is seen that *you* have condescended to ask her to dance."

Addison, whose wits were ordinarily quite as needle-sharp as were hers, received this piece of shameless flattery with entire complacency, and upon the set's ending and Lord Langmere's bringing Kitty to Cressida, since Lady Constance had already disappeared into the card-room, he graciously bestowed upon Kitty the desired accolade of soliciting her hand for the country dance that was to follow. As he led her off into the set, Cressida was importuned in turn by Lord Langmere and no fewer than three other gentlemen to allow them to do the same for her, but she denied them all for the moment.

"There is someone I must speak to first," she said. "Yes, you may have the boulanger, Leonard, and each of you"—to her three other swains—"a waltz, but now do bring that very tall, fair young man standing so mournfully against the wall over there to me. His name is Captain Miles Harries."

The youngest of her admirers dutifully went off, and Lord Langmere looked at her with an enquiring smile.

"Harries?" he said.

"Yes," said Cressida. "I met him the other day in Octavius Mayr's office, and he is a lamb, but a very uncomfortable one just now, I am afraid. You must be very kind to him, Leonard, because Addison has just told me in a horrid, blighting way that he is not *quite* the thing, and he is sure to be roundly snubbed if someone does not take him in hand. Oh, Captain Harries, how nice to see you again!" she went on, holding out her hand to the bashful Captain as he came up. "This is Lord Langmere, who is going to take you off presently to the refreshment saloon, where you may have champagne and lobster patties, which are the very best reason, I think, for attending any ball. But first you must come and sit down with me, and tell me what you think of us all."

She led the way to a small gilt sofa set along the wall, out of the way of the dancers, and Captain Harries followed her obediently, but with the look upon his face of a young subaltern going into action for the first time and terrified, not of the danger, but of the possibility of doing something to disgrace his uniform.

"You aren't afraid of me, are you?" Cressida asked, as he sat down beside her on the edge of the sofa. "I know I must have given you a very poor opinion of me that morning in Octavius Mayr's office, but I do assure you I am not always so shockingly rag-mannered. That was only because of Dev. I expect you are a great friend of his and never quarrel with him, but we began our acquaintance by coming to cuffs and I am afraid we always will."

She was then vexed with herself for bringing Rossiter's name into the conversation, convinced herself that Captain Harries would certainly believe she had desired this tête-à-tête only for the purpose of talking of him, and assumed an air of such coolness that her companion had only the courage to say in a rather abashed way that he and Dev had not quarrelled more than once that he could remember, and that, perhaps, didn't really signify, because it had only been over a bottle of very poor red wine.

"A bottle of wine?" said Cressida, looking interested and forgetting her vexation.

"Yes," explained the Captain seriously. "You see, there wasn't any more to be had and I dropped it, but I shouldn't have done if he hadn't jogged my elbow. It was in Portugal, and a very thirsty day," he added, as if that must make everything perfectly clear.

The picture his words conjured up of the dashing current hero of the London *ton* and the fair young giant beside her squabbling like a pair of schoolboys over a broken bottle of cheap red wine was too much for Cressida; she burst out laughing and Captain Harries, looking surprised but a good deal relieved, gave her a rather sheepish grin.

"You must come to Mount Street very soon—perhaps tomorrow?" Cressida said, "and tell me all about your adventures. One can't talk properly at a ball. Were you at Waterloo? Or had you sold out before that?"

"Yes; Dev and I both sold out in '14, after Boney had been rompéd and sent to Elba," said Captain Harries. "You see, Dev had been in India and he wanted to go back—"

"For those fabulous rubies—of course!" Cressida said. "I wish you will tell me all about them tomorrow. I shall be the envy of all my friends if I am the only one of them to know the whole story—unless, of course, Dev decides to spread the tale himself this evening. I understand he *is* to put in an appearance here?"

"Yes—or I shouldn't be here myself!" the Captain said with a rueful grin. "Nor even have been invited! I've told him, there's no need for him to drag me into it when he is going into Society, for I'm like a cat on a hot bakestone in a place like this—"

"Nonsense!" said Cressida roundly. "You may enjoy

yourself here as well as anywhere else in London. I daresay there is not a man here who is not envying you your
adventures, to say nothing of those very broad shoulders
that cast their own pitiful padded ones quite in the shade!
And as for the young ladies—do you care for dancing? I
am sure I can introduce you to any number of pretty girls
who will be happy to stand up with you."

A slight flush crept unexpectedly into the Captain's
face, and his blue eyes went to the ballroom floor, linger-
ing there, it seemed, upon one particular dancer.

"Yes, there is—that is, I *should* like you to introduce me to—to one young lady," he stammered, with an
air of some self-consciousness. "The—the young lady
who came with you this evening—"

"Miss Chenevix? But of course!" said Cressida cor-
dially. "She will be delighted! She is only just arrived in
London, you see, and is as little acquainted here as yourself, for she has lived almost all her life in Devonshire."

Captain Harries, almost interrupting her in his
pleasure at the coincidence, said he came from Devonshire himself, and, apparently deciding at about this moment that Cressida was to be considered as friend and
not enemy, relaxed sufficiently to talk to her in a quite
easy way about his home near Plymouth, and how he
hoped in time to become well enough off, owing to his
association with Rossiter, to buy a respectable property
in that neighbourhood and settle down to a country life.

"I'm not in the least like Dev, you know," he confided to her. "In fact, I can't for the life of me see why he
chooses to put up with me, except that we've been in a
fair number of tight places together and—well, we've always stood by each other. But *he* is at home to a peg anywhere he goes, whether it's Calcutta or Rio de Janeiro or
London, and there's no saying, you know, how high he
may go if he likes. Why, he might marry the daughter of
a duke!"

Cressida, with a quite inexplicably disagreeable

feeling somewhere inside her, was about to enquire if Rossiter had any particular duke's daughter in mind when Captain Harries, his face suddenly brightening, exclaimed, "But here he is now!" and Cressida, following his gaze, saw Rossiter himself, his tall figure showing to excellent advantage in evening-dress which, though entirely fashionable, displayed no affectations of dandyism, standing in the doorway, surveying the brilliant scene before him with something of the cool detachment of a hawk looking over an assemblage of fowls.

CHAPTER 5

It was not to be expected that the lion of the evening would be allowed to progress farther than the doorway of the ballroom before becoming a centre of attention, and Cressida anticipated that her own meeting with him would be long postponed, or—if fortune were with her—not take place at all in the crush of guests crowding the rooms of Dalingridge House.

But she had reckoned without the lion himself—or, it might be more accurate to say, without the hawk, to use the simile that had occurred to her as she had seen him standing in the doorway. For as that keen-eyed predator leisurely selects its victim from its airy circling flight, so Rossiter, from his superior height, gazed around over the lesser heads of the persons clustered about him until, espying *his* victim across the room, he clove a ruthless way through them, with scarcely an apology, towards his object.

As for Cressida, it was not until he was almost upon her that she realised *she* was that object.

"Hallo, Miles!" he greeted Captain Harries. "I see you've found your feet: didn't I tell you you would? Miss

Calverton"—he bowed slightly, giving her his wry, sardonic smile—"I hope I see you in better temper this evening than on the occasion of our last meeting. And now may I request the honour of standing up with you for the next dance?"

Cressida frankly stared at him. "I *don't* see why you should care to, after that last meeting!" she said. "But if you are really serious—and I am strongly inclined to doubt that you are!—I may thankfully inform you that I am already engaged."

"You are always engaged, it appears!" said Rossiter, regarding her provocatively. "To Lord Langmere this time?"

"Yes, to Lord Langmere—but *not* in the way you are hinting!" said Cressida, wondering why it was that Rossiter could always manage to set her hackles up to the extent that she quite forgot her manners. "Only for the next dance."

"A pity! I had expected you would have made quicker work of him. Very well, then. The dance after that."

"I am very much afraid," said Cressida sweetly, but with dangerously glinting eyes, "that I am *engaged* for that as well."

"And for the next, and the next, and the next, I daresay," said Rossiter affably. "Not being dull of understanding, Miss Calverton, I take your meaning. To put it in the plainest possible terms, you do not care to dance with me."

"To put it in the plainest possible terms, Captain Rossiter, you are quite correct!"

By this time the set had ended and, Lady Constance being still in the card-room, Addison brought Kitty across the floor to Cressida, at the same moment that Lord Langmere appeared to claim his dance. Cressida, who knew that neither Addison nor Langmere was acquainted with Rossiter, was obliged to perform the introductions, which she did in a decidedly offhand manner. She then realised that she had quite unaccountably neglected to present Rossiter and Harries to Kitty, and was about to do so when Rossiter himself, his eyes fixed upon Miss Chenevix in what appeared to be cool but definite admiration, called her attention to this omission.

"Good!" he said, when she had pronounced the necessary social formula. "It wouldn't have done, you see, for me to have asked Miss Chenevix to dance with me before she had received my credentials as an old acquaintance of yours in good standing, Miss Calverton." He addressed Kitty with an air of negligent gallantry. "May I have the honour, Miss Chenevix—?"

Kitty cast a dutifully questioning glance at Cressida, but she so obviously wished to accept the invitation that had been tendered to her that Cressida, under penalty of causing a small, significant scene under Addison's eyes, was obliged to nod her assent. Rossiter thereupon walked off with Kitty on his arm, while Addison, his brows raised over his cold blue eyes, gazed interrogatively at Cressida.

"An *old acquaintance* of yours, Cressy?" he enquired. "You are being very sly, are you not, my love? One would never have gathered, when we were discussing the gallant Captain a short while ago, that you were an *old acquaintance* of his."

"It was a very brief acquaintanceship, I assure you," Cressida said, and quite despairing, after her own imprudence in speaking of the matter to both Lady Constance and Langmere, of being able to keep from Addison's inquisitiveness the facts of that acquaintanceship, added, "Only long enough for us to plight our troth and then unplight it again, which, you know, my dear, to a green girl is a matter of weeks—no more. Leonard, had we not best join the set—?"

Lord Langmere, who, following her instructions,

had been talking kindly to Captain Harries, thus depriving the latter of the opportunity to ask Kitty to dance before Rossiter had snatched her up from under his nose, said so they had, and they went off together, leaving Captain Harries behind with the Honourable Mr. Addison, who cast a cold glance upon him and then also walked away.

"I *do* wish I had not been obliged to present Rossiter to Kitty," Cressida said in a vexed tone to Langmere as they took their places in the set. "He is not at all the sort of man for a young girl to know—but then I daresay it does not signify in the end. He will certainly not make *her* the object of his gallantry."

And she put the matter out of her mind, until at the end of the set she was startled to see that Rossiter, instead of bringing Kitty back to her, was standing amicably chatting with her, resisting the blandishments of Lady Dalingridge, who wished to parade her captive lion before her guests, and that he apparently had every intention of standing up with Miss Chenevix for the next set as well.

"Devil!" thought Cressida, her indignation mounting once more. "He is only doing it because he thinks it will annoy me!"

But again there was nothing she could do without provoking an undesirable small scene, so she allowed her own partner to lead her into the set, privately determining to get Kitty's ear at its conclusion and inform her of the extreme inadvisability of a young girl's making herself conspicuous by standing up twice in one evening with a man of Rossiter's reputation.

As it happened, however, she was spared the necessity of instructing Kitty upon this point by the arrival upon the scene, just as the set was ending, of a breathless Lady Constance, who, it appeared, had been routed out of the pleasures of a gossipping game of whist in the

card-room by a well-meaning dowager who said she was
sure she would wish to know that Miss Chenevix had
stood up for two dances in a row with Captain Rossiter,
and that Dolly Dalingridge was quite livid with disappointment because she had not been able to exchange
more than two words with him herself and was telling
everyone that she knew nothing at all about Kitty, but
that one could see she had been brought up without
proper principles.

"And I *did* so depend upon *you*, dearest Cressy,"
Lady Constance said, the very aigrette on her turban
quivering with reproach, "to see to it that she didn't fall
into the briars, because she is *quite* inexperienced, you
know, and didn't so much as realise, until I warned her
of it, that she must on no account waltz in public without
the permission of one of the Patronesses of Almack's!
There! Thank goodness, the set is ending! Of course I
have never met Captain Rossiter, but I shall most certainly give him a piece of my mind if he is bold enough to
ask poor little Kitty to stand up with him for a third time!"

And she hurried off, to be shortly seen snatching
Kitty away from an amused Rossiter in a very high-
handed sort of way, which would have convinced anyone
of the genuineness of her claim to Plantagenet blood.

Lord Langmere, who happened to have been standing beside Cressida when this bit of by-play had taken
place, and had watched it with mild interest, now remarked to her that it rather appeared to him that Lady
Constance was making a piece of work over nothing.

"As a matter of fact," he said, "she may even be
doing your little Miss Chenevix a disservice. Rossiter is
obviously attracted by the girl, and if he should have decided at this point in his life to settle himself—which
seems possible, by his return to England—he would be a
rich prize indeed for a penniless young girl to capture."

"Rossiter! You cannot be serious!" Cressida turned

an astonished face upon him. "A man of his—his *experi-ence*, to use the politest term, to marry a girl scarcely out of the schoolroom! He would be bored to death in a week, and she—" She shook her head decisively. "No, it is quite absurd! This is only one of his sudden freaks. He was piqued because I would not grant him a dance, and this is his way of being revenged upon me!"

"Of course, you may be right," Lord Langmere conceded, but looking unconvinced. "A very thoughtless and ill-judged revenge it would be, though, my dear, to single out a young girl and make her the object of expectations that he has no intention of satisfying. Is he such a paltry fellow? I have only just met him, but he does not appear so to me."

"Yes—*no!*" Cressida said, obliged to swallow the indignation that had prompted her first reply and give Rossiter his due. "He is not ordinarily devious, I believe. But this—" She stopped speaking suddenly, seeing that Rossiter, once more shaking off the importunities of Lady Dalingridge, who had again attempted to seize upon him as he had been relinquished by Lady Constance, was purposefully approaching. "Oh, good heavens! Here he comes! What now?" she said quickly. "Leonard, if he means to ask me to go down to supper with him, I am already engaged to you—do you understand?"

Lord Langmere said gallantly that it would please him above all things to take her down to supper, as it was for the purpose of asking her to allow him that pleasure that he had just approached her; and then Rossiter was upon them.

"Well, Cressy?" he said in a quizzing tone, regarding her slightly flushed and highly unwelcoming countenance. "I knew I was engaging in a forlorn hope, but just how forlorn it is I can see by your face, before I have so much as made my request. You are firmly determined, I gather, to eat with me no more than you will dance with me."

Cressida, assuming an air of indifference, shrugged and glanced at Langmere.

"As I daresay you have already guessed, I am *engaged* to Lord Langmere for supper," she said pointedly. "And may I *particularly* request," she added on a sudden unworthy impulse, which she would certainly have quelled if it had not been for the unwonted perturbation that had brought the colour to her face when she had seen Rossiter approaching her, "that you do not ask Miss Chenevix to go down with you? She is in a way under my charge at present, as she is living under my roof, and I may tell you that I consider you have already drawn quite enough undesirable notice upon her by asking her to stand up with you twice this evening."

"Do you, by God!" Cressida's eyes, which had been purposely fixed upon her fan—a pretty thing of frosted crape on ivory sticks—flew up, startled, to his dark face. A slight flush of anger had risen in it, and as she stared at him he continued harshly, "You are responsible for your own actions and inclinations, my girl, but when you try to make yourself responsible for mine as well, let me tell you that you have gone your length! I shall neither be guided by you nor make myself accountable to you in what I do. If Miss Chenevix's guardians choose to consider me an unsuitable person for her to know, I shall take the matter up with them; but what *you* have to do with it—beyond a wish to meddle in what is none of your affair—escapes my understanding!"

And he turned and strode off without another word. Lord Langmere, who had been a somewhat uncomfortable auditor to this exchange, was moved at this point to say fair-mindedly but rather unwisely to Cressida, "Really, my dear, he was quite in the right, you know. The matter rests in Lady Con's hands, and I am sure she has said everything that is necessary."

"Oh, of course—being a man, you take *his* part!" flashed Cressida still more unworthily, and, clasping the fragile ivory sticks of her fan so tightly that she felt some of them break between her fingers, she too walked quickly away.

Naturally, being aware that she had acted badly, she was very gay indeed with her next partner, one of the German princelings whom Addison had despised, flirting with him in such a dashing manner that Addison began to speculate seriously on whether his suggestion that she might become a *Prinzessin* had really taken root in her mind, and causing several of the more proper dowagers present to remark to one another that really, my dear, if Cressida Calverton did not mend her ways, everyone would be saying that she was *fast*.

Meanwhile, Rossiter had gone straight across the room to where Lady Constance, having secured an eligible if not exciting partner for Kitty in the person of the very young and bashful third son of a baronet, had seated herself beside one of those same censorious dowagers upon a small gilt rout chair, having determined to keep vigilant watch over her charge during the remainder of the evening. Cressida, who, although appearing wholly absorbed in her flirtation with her princeling, was perfectly aware of Rossiter's movements, was astonished to see him halt before Lady Constance's chair and, after parleying for a few moments with her and her companion, promptly draw up a third chair and seat himself beside them. The two middle-aged ladies, she could see, were making a valiant attempt to maintain their air of virtuous disapproval in the face of this frontal attack by the Captain; but they were no more immune than would the young ladies they were chaperoning have been to the flattery of having been so pointedly singled out by the lion of the evening, and they were soon smiling and engaging in what appeared to be a very comfortable conversation *à trois.*

The set ended; Cressida was claimed by Lord Langmere, who came, as he had promised, to take her down to supper; and the next she saw of Rossiter he was, astoundingly, seated in the supper-room in a group comprising Lady Constance and the dowager to whom he had been talking in the ballroom, the dowager's daughter, Captain Harries, Kitty, and the now perfectly tongue-tied third son of a baronet who had been dancing with her.

"Birds of a feather," said Addison, pausing beside the chair in which Lord Langmere had installed Cressida while he went to fill a plate for her, "do *not*, it appears, always flock together. I refer, my dear Cressy, to your friend Captain Rossiter and that extraordinarily motley crew he has gathered round him. Three sucking babes, a pair of dowagers, and poor Captain Harries, who is regarding your Miss Chenevix rather as if he were a devout Muslim discovering his first houri at the gates of Paradise. If I am mixing my metaphors rather badly, it is because I have been reduced to a state of utter confusion by this grouping. Can you explain it to me? Dolly, I fear, is about to scratch Lady Con's eyes out with jealousy, and in point of fact I believe it may well come to pistols at twenty paces on Paddington Green between them if Lady Con does not relinquish Rossiter to her soon."

To Cressida's relief, Lord Langmere's arrival at that moment with a pair of plates abundantly heaped with the creams, aspics, and Chantillies provided for her guests by Lady Dalingridge prevented her from answering this speech directly, and she applied herself assiduously to her plate while Addison and several other members of her coterie who had also stopped beside her chair on their way to the buffet made witty conversation over their hostess's disappointment and Rossiter's odd choice of supper companions.

Her own mind was in a puzzle. Could it be possible, she asked herself, that Rossiter had indeed been so taken by Kitty that he was willing to endure what must be the decidedly dull conversation of his present companions for the sake of being near her? The girl was well enough, certainly, and she as certainly appeared to advantage that evening in the shimmering spider-gauze gown; but she was not a Beauty, and her quiet style of good looks was not the sort to strike a man like a *coup de foudre*.

The only feasible explanation of the situation appeared to be the one presented to her earlier by Lord Langmere—that Rossiter's intention in returning to England had been to settle himself in life, and that for this purpose he was looking about him as expeditiously as possible for a suitable bride.

That this explanation was also looming large in Lady Constance's mind was made evident to Cressida as soon as they were all seated in Lord Langmere's carriage on their way back to Mount Street at the end of the ball. She was full of Kitty's success that evening—"If you will believe it, my dear, outside of the waltzes, which of course I would not permit her to stand up for, she was obliged to sit out only two dances!"—and in particular of Rossiter, who, from being a monster intent upon ruining Kitty's reputation, had become "a most delightful man, such odd, abrupt manners but truly a most interesting conversationalist! And so taken with Kitty! Indeed, he complimented me on her being such an agreeable girl, not at all *coming*, like so many modern young ladies— not that *I* could take credit for that, and so I told him, though of course it *was* I who had instructed her as to how she was to conduct herself at a London ball."

Lord Langmere, living up to his reputation as a good-humoured man, said that he was sure Miss Chenevix had quite deserved her success, and that he himself had very much enjoyed his own dance with her. Kitty smiled at him—was it, Cressida wondered suddenly, that little smile, so modest and self-deprecating, that had taken Rossiter in that roomful of chattering, flaunting females?—but said nothing. The girl had been gazing out the window of the carriage at the London streets, which looked very dark and full of inky shadows in spite of the flaring light cast by the new gas lamps, and Cressida, watching her, imagined there was a thoughtful expression upon her fragile, fair face.

The conversation continued on Rossiter, but Kitty herself added nothing to it except for an occasional dutiful, "Yes, indeed, ma'am," in reply to one of Lady Constance's questions; and only as the carriage halted in Mount Street and the footman sprang down from his perch behind to let down the steps for them to descend did an unsolicited remark fall from her lips.

"He is very rich—isn't he?" she asked in a quiet, abstracted voice, addressing Lady Constance.

"Oh, my dear, yes—rich enough to buy an Abbey, if one can credit all one hears!" Lady Constance said promptly; and then, in a confusion of trailing gowns, evening mantles, and reticules, the three ladies, assisted by Lord Langmere, descended from the carriage and went inside.

CHAPTER 6

"I expect," said Lady Constance to Cressida with some satisfaction over the breakfast-table the next morning, "that we shall have Rossiter calling here today. He asked me last evening if he might, and, as taken as he appeared to be with Kitty, I daresay he will not let the grass grow under his feet. She is altering that blue jaconet muslin carriage-dress you gave her at this very moment, in the event he should ask her to go for a drive with him. I told her Moodle might very well do it for her, but you know how she dislikes making additional work for the servants. Really, it is scarcely to be wondered at that Rossiter finds her so very attractive! Her manners so captivating—simple and composed, with not the least hint of missishness, which you know always puts gentlemen off. And she attends with such interest to what one is saying—"

"What *did* Rossiter find to say to her?" Cressida broke in to ask, for in truth this matter had given her mind a considerable amount of occupation during the unaccountably wakeful hours she had spent before she had at last fallen asleep the night before. "I should think they must have nothing in common."

"Not a bit of it," said Lady Constance superbly. "Kitty has an excellent understanding, and is quite capable of taking an interest in any topic a gentleman may choose to discuss with her. And I must say that it is not at all difficult to do so when Captain Rossiter is on the subject of the new steam railways, which he says will quite replace horses in the future. I well remember my dear Jeremy taking me to see Mr. Trevithick's *Catch me who can* when it was exhibited here in London some years ago, though of course I understood nothing of the principle upon which it ran when he tried to explain it to me. But I am persuaded that Kitty will understand perfectly if Rossiter ever attempts to explain it to *her*."

It was on the tip of Cressida's tongue to say that Kitty would certainly give an excellent *performance* of a young lady perfectly understanding even the most abstruse details of anything Rossiter chose to explain to her; but she bit the words back, surprised and half ashamed that she should so much as have formulated them in her mind. She had no reason, she told herself, to believe that Kitty was dissembling in anything she said or did, whether in regard to Rossiter or upon any other matter; and yet the girl's quiet words as they had descended from the carriage the night before—"He is very rich—isn't he?"—still lingered disagreeably in her mind.

She could not prevent herself from feeling that all Kitty's interest in Rossiter lay in those words—and why should it not? she asked herself irritably. Kitty would not be the first penniless girl to look prudently for the fortune involved before she gave her heart: every young female was not so rash as Cressy Calverton had been when she had bestowed her affections, without a thought for the future, upon an impecunious soldier.

Meanwhile, Lady Constance, quite unaware that she had lost her audience, was continuing upon her subject, debating with herself when it might be convenient for Kitty to have the carriage to convey her to Hans Town to visit her aunt Mills—"for she does not wish to be backward in any attention to her, of course, and it would be only proper for her to call and enquire as to her aunt's present state of health, now that she is in London. Really, I cannot help but think, after last night, that it was truly providential that Mrs. Mills *was* taken ill so inconveniently, for if Kitty had been with *her* she would never have received a card to the Dalingridges' ball and have met Captain Rossiter. It is as I always say—such things are *meant*. And I am sure dear Kitty deserves any good fortune that may come to her on the head of it."

Cressida, who had by this time had quite enough of Kitty, Mrs. Mills, *and* Rossiter, said hastily that Kitty might have the carriage that very afternoon if it suited her and escaped from the table, hoping that she might go upstairs, don her hat and gloves, and be out of the house upon a round of morning-calls before Rossiter—if indeed Lady Constance was correct in her assessment of his intentions—appeared upon the doorstep.

But her luck was quite out, for just as she was descending the staircase the knocker sounded, and she arrived in the hall below precisely as Harbage trod across its black-and-white lozenge floor and admitted Rossiter.

He saw her at once and, abandoning his curly-brimmed beaver and stick to Harbage, came forward towards her.

"An unexpected piece of ill fortune, my arriving at this moment," he said coolly, as if reading her mind. "No doubt you would have denied yourself if we had not chanced to meet in this way, or, better still"—regarding her hat and gloves—"you would have been out of the house altogether and have been under no necessity to see me. But you needn't vex yourself: I have not called to see you, but Miss Chenevix."

Cressida, who had been, after a night's chastening reflection, reluctantly prepared to acknowledge that she had acted badly the previous evening and to behave towards Rossiter with proper civility when next she encountered him, stiffened at this sardonic greeting.

"Miss Chenevix is abovestairs, I believe," she said coldly, quite forgetting all her good resolutions in a moment. "Harbage will inform her that you are here. Will you go into the drawing room until she comes down?"

"I should prefer it to being frozen to death here," Rossiter said frankly, as Harbage went off. "Unless, of course, you intend to continue the chilling process there until Miss Chenevix appears?" His manner altered abruptly. "Good God, Cressy, can we never meet without coming to dagger-drawing with each other?" he demanded, frowning. "That business between us has been over and done with these seven years—"

"Good morning, Captain Rossiter," said a quiet voice above them. Cressida and Rossiter looked up to see Kitty walking down the stairs toward them, a smile of pleasure upon her face. "How kind of you to call!" she went on, holding out her hand to Rossiter rather shyly as she reached the foot of the stairs, and then glancing, as if in slight uncertainty, towards Cressida. "I believe, though, that Miss Calverton is just on the point of going out—"

"I have not come to see Miss Calverton, but to ask *you* to go for a drive with me," Rossiter said promptly. "I have a new team I am trying this morning—Welsh-bred greys—and it occurred to me that, since it is such a splendid day, you might enjoy driving into the country, to Richmond Park, perhaps."

"Oh, I should like it above all things!" Kitty said at once. And then, breaking off and looking questioningly at Cressida, "That is," she emended, "if there is nothing that Miss Calverton wishes me to do for her instead—"

"Nonsense! What should there be?" Cressida said briskly. "You are in London to enjoy yourself, so you must do whatever pleases you. Captain Rossiter, I shall bid you good morning."

And she walked out the front door and down the steps to her waiting carriage, trying to stifle the captious thought that Kitty had come down the stairs with such suspicious promptness as to suggest she had not needed Harbage's announcement to inform her of Rossiter's arrival, having been on the watch for it from her window, and that, furthermore, she had been so well prepared to accept his offer to take her for a drive, in spite of that deferential little speech offering to forego her own pleasure at a word from Cressida, that she had already donned the blue jaconet muslin carriage-dress she had just been altering.

Cressida was about to step into her barouche when the sound of another vehicle approaching caused her to look up, and she saw Captain Harries reining in a smart phaeton before her door. She waited on the flagway as he handed his reins to his groom and then, jumping down quickly, came over to greet her.

"Good morning!" she said, smiling up at him. "Have you come to call upon us? You must be disappointed then, I fear! As you see, I am off to pay some morning-calls myself, and Miss Chenevix, too, is on the point of driving to Richmond Park with Captain Rossiter." She saw the quick shadow that crossed his face and said on impulse, "If you would care to, Captain Harries, why not come with me? I am not planning to visit any formidable great ladies this morning, but only a very agreeable friend of mine who lives all year in the country and will talk to you of nothing but horses, and then I must go on to see another lady who was a godchild of my great-aunt's and whom I have not clapped eyes on in a dozen years—strictly a duty call, and you may support me if it chances that *she* is insupportably dull!"

Captain Harries, who was well aware, after the observations he had made at last evening's ball, that the invitation Miss Calverton had just extended to him would be considered extremely flattering by a great many gentlemen of far more exalted position than his own, stammered that he would be honoured.

"Good! Come into my carriage then," Cressida said, issuing an order to one of her footmen to see that the Captain's own phaeton was properly taken care of. Captain Harries handed her into the barouche, and was in the act of seating himself beside her when the front door of the house opened once more and Kitty, now wearing bonnet and gloves, emerged, accompanied by Rossiter. A quick flush came up in Captain Harries's face, while at the same time it seemed to Cressida that a flash of displeasure appeared momentarily in Rossiter's eyes as he perceived that his friend had already apparently got upon such intimate terms with her as to be carried off captive in her carriage.

"Good heavens, can he really be so idiotish as to believe I am deliberately getting up a flirtation with Captain Harries, and mean to turn his head, or drive him to dissipation, or whatever it is that unscrupulous females are presumed to do to innocent young men?" she thought, with some indignation upon her own part, and told the coachman to drive on without allowing Rossiter time to approach the carriage.

As a result of this notion she spoke very kindly to Captain Harries as they drove through the busy London streets, but so firmly in the tone of a more experienced elder sister that Captain Harries, who had several older sisters of his own, felt quite at ease with her, and before long was confiding in her with even less reserve than he had done the previous evening at the ball.

"You can't think what a difference it makes to find

that someone like you, who is at the very top of the trees—oh, yes, I've learned *that* much by time!—is such a—well, such a regular right 'un," he said ingenuously, which made Cressida laugh and tell him if he ever found himself in the briars because of someone who *wasn't* a regular right 'un to come to her and she would help him to extricate himself with the least possible amount of trouble.

"Thank you, Miss Calverton," said the Captain, who was really grateful because he saw that, in spite of the laughter, she meant what she said. "But if you mean in Society, I don't think I'll stay in it long enough to fall into the briars. I only came up to London to please Dev, and I'd be thinking of going back to Devonshire now if it weren't for—"

He broke off abruptly, his fair face colouring warmly.

"If it weren't for Miss Chenevix?" Cressida finished it for him lightly. "Dev seems to have stolen a march on you there, doesn't he? But never mind; it is early days still, and I am sure if you set your mind to it you will be able to cut him out. Your manners are far more agreeable than his, you know!"

The barouche was drawing up at that moment before a narrow house in Half Moon Street, and the Captain's inarticulate words of protest over his having either the power or the wish to step between his friend and any young lady for whom he might be forming an attachment were lost in the bustle of descending from the carriage. Inside the house Captain Harries found himself, as Cressida had predicted, immediately involved in horse-talk with his young and handsome hostess, and, after a very agreeable half hour spent in this fashion, was able to face the succeeding call with a great deal more equanimity than he would have believed possible when he had set out from Mount Street with Cressida a short time before.

The second call, however, which was in Keppel

Street, turned out to be rather less in his line than the first, for the hostess and all her morning-callers were respectably middle-aged or elderly ladies, who talked to one another confidentially about their respective illnesses and looked rather askance at the sight of such a very large young man invading what the Captain was mentally characterising as their hen-roost. To his relief, the conversation seemed to be of no greater interest to Cressida than it was to him, and after paying her devoirs formally to Mrs. Torrance, their hostess, she cast him a glance indicating that she was prepared to take her departure, when the arrival of a new caller and the round of introductions it entailed momentarily put a halt to her intention.

The new arrival was a sensible-looking woman of some five-and-forty years, wearing a slightly outmoded frock and bonnet, and she was introduced to the company as Mrs. Mills, an old schoolfellow of Mrs. Torrance. Cressida, idly noting that the name was the same as that of Kitty's aunt, wondered if there was a connexion, but thought not, since the name was a common one; there were undoubtedly, she considered, dozens of Millses living in London.

She could not fail to note, however, that the pronouncing of her own name appeared to call up an expression of considerable interest to Mrs. Mills's face, and before she could properly carry out her intention of leaving, the lady herself had come across the room and taken a chair beside her.

"It *is* Miss *Cressida* Calverton—is it not?" she enquired. And, as Cressida nodded in slight surprise, "I thought I could not be mistaken," she went on with a smile, "although Selina did not mention your Christian name. I am Kitty's aunt, you see, and you must allow me to thank you—as I am sure Kitty has already done herself—for your great kindness towards her. I was quite prepared, naturally, to bring her out myself, but the advantages *I* could give her were slight indeed compared to those she will receive from *your* patronage, and Lady Constance's. I can only hope that she appreciates her good fortune—but there!" she added comfortably, "knowing dear Kitty, I am quite sure that she does. Such a quiet, sensible girl—don't you find her so?"

She looked at Cressida, as if expecting some reply, and Cressida, swiftly collecting herself, said automatically, "Yes, indeed!" She was still, however, too surprised by the revelation that appeared to be contained in Mrs. Mills's words to be able to prevent herself from enquiring involuntarily, "But—you have made a very rapid recovery, have you not, ma'am? I understand you have been ill—"

"Ill?" It was now Mrs. Mills's turn to look surprised. "Why, no," she said. "Where can you have had that idea? I am happy to say that I enjoy excellent health." She looked affectionately across the room towards Mrs. Torrance. "No doubt you have misunderstood something that Selina has said," she remarked, "which scarcely surprises me, for she is always in such poor twig that she is forever fidgeting herself that there may be something amiss with her friends as well."

Cressida, who felt that this was neither the time nor the place to inform Mrs. Mills that her belief that she had been ill had been founded, not upon some vague words let fall by Mrs. Torrance, but upon the extremely specific statements repeatedly made by Kitty herself, was silent, and after a few more words of conventional gratitude uttered by Mrs. Mills on the subject of her kindness in sponsoring Kitty's come-out, Cressida seized the opportunity to escape. But her head was in a whirl: in spite of her previous suspicions of Kitty's sincerity, she could scarcely believe that the girl had been guilty of the calculating deception that Mrs. Mills's words had innocently revealed to her.

And yet there was no room left for doubt: Kitty *must* have written that first appealing letter to Lady Constance in the full knowledge that Mrs. Mills was both in excellent health and perfectly willing to sponsor her come-out in London. It had been a gamble to write it, certainly, for there had always been the chance that, in spite of the fact that Mrs. Mills did not move in the same circles as did Cressida and Lady Constance, some contretemps such as had occurred that morning at Mrs. Torrance's might discover her lie. But it was a risk, it seemed, that Miss Kitty Chenevix had been coolly prepared to take in the interests of her ambition, and it had apparently been so easy for her to pull the wool over her mother's eyes and convince *her* that Lady Constance's offer had been made spontaneously, rather than as the result of an appeal from her, that no doubt she had felt quite secure in the success of her deception when she had arrived in London.

Cressida, still deep in thought, mounted into her barouche and ordered her coachman to drive back to Mount Street, and only as Captain Harries seated himself beside her did she come to herself sufficiently to realise that she was not alone.

"Oh, I *am* sorry!" she said, turning to him with the best attempt at a smile of which she was capable at the moment. "The truth is, I have been wool-gathering—"

She broke off, a trifle surprised to find the Captain regarding her with a very serious expression upon his own face, as if he quite shared her concern over the dilemma into which Mrs. Mills's words had plunged her. He had, of course, she realised now, been seated close enough to her while Mrs. Mills had been speaking to her to overhear all that was being said, but it did not seem to her that the conversation could have offered any clue to an outsider of the real situation, or of her own astonishment and—yes, she was ready to admit it, anger—when she had discovered how neatly she had been tricked by young Miss Chenevix.

But that impression of an unexpected native shrewdness in the Captain's character that she had had upon her first meeting with him was strengthened now as he said to her in a quiet, troubled voice, "It is about Miss Chenevix—isn't it? You were very much surprised when Mrs. Mills told you she had not been ill—"

"Was I? Well, perhaps!" Cressida said, interrupting him with an attempt at lightness. "It really seems I am quite muddle-headed today! I don't know what poor Mrs. Mills must have thought—"

"I am glad to say I don't believe she thought what I am thinking," Captain Harries said in the same thoughtful undertone, and he continued at once, "Not to beat about the bush, Miss Calverton—it was Miss Chenevix who told you that her aunt was ill, wasn't it? And that is why it is you and Lady Constance, instead of Mrs. Mills, who are bringing her out this Season—"

Cressida looked at him in astonished respect.

"You are really an extraordinary man, Captain Harries!" she said. "To have gathered so much from those few words—"

"It is because I take a very great interest in Miss Chenevix," the Captain said simply. "I don't think I should ordinarily have been so acute." He looked at her with anxiety visible in his frank blue eyes. "I expect it has made you very angry with her," he said, "and I can't blame you for that, but I hope you will try to make allowances, Miss Calverton. She is—very young, you know, and—and I daresay it seemed a great opportunity to her—"

"Yes, I am sure it did, for her to have taken such a risk!" Cressida said, shrugging. "Very young and—very ambitious, you might add, Captain Harries!"

"And what, please, do you intend to do about it?"
Captain Harries's eyes were asking her when she looked
over at him again—a question, she saw, that he did not
dare to put into words; and, touched by this evidence of
love at first sight, and clinging to it buckle and thong in
spite of clear evidence of its object's unworthiness, she
laid her hand lightly upon his for a moment.

"Pray don't fret yourself over it!" she said reassur-
ingly. "I am not such a dragon as to send her home in disgrace. I shan't, in fact, even tell her of the discovery I
have made; it would make living in the same house far
too uncomfortable! But I shan't try to hide from you that
it *must* make a difference in my feelings towards her. I
don't care for duplicity, and I have learned that when
you have discovered it in someone in one instance, you
are very likely to find it repeated."

The Captain looked unhappy, but said nothing to
attempt to refute her statement; and Cressida, reflecting somewhat cynically upon love's ability to be blind to
the obvious when seeing it would besmirch the beloved
object, was left to her own thoughts until the carriage
arrived back in Mount Street.

By that time she had decided that it would certainly
not do, since she had promised Captain Harries not to
bring Kitty to book for her deception, to disclose anything at all about the matter to Lady Constance, who
could assuredly not be trusted to keep it to herself, and
as a result she was obliged to endure more of that lady's
raptures upon Kitty's character and conquests as they
met in Cressida's dressing room later in the day.

"And you will never guess who called upon her this
morning while you were out!" Lady Constance remarked
impressively. "Addison—yes, my dear, no less! Of
course he made a pretence of having called to see you and
me, but it was quite obvious, when I told him Kitty was
gone to Richmond Park with Captain Rossiter, how the

matter stood. He was quite venomous about Rossiter—you know that waspish tongue of his!—and said Dolly Dalingridge was so angry with him for neglecting her last evening that she was going all over London this morning asking her friends to cut him from their invitation lists."

"As if Rossiter would care a groat if they did!" Cressida said, shrugging. "They won't, though—not as long as everyone in London is still talking of him."

"Yes, but if Addison has taken one of his dislikes to him, he may do a great deal to turn people against him," Lady Constance pointed out. "You know what an influence he has, and it will be all the greater now if this extraordinary tale going the rounds today—you *have* heard it, I expect?—that Brummell has been obliged to flee the country because of his debts, should turn out to be true. The man will have half of London trembling at his frown—"

"Yes, indeed—mushroom gentlemen, trumped-up April-squires, halflings aspiring to be dandies!" Cressida said scornfully. "Good God, Lady Con, you are not seriously suggesting that Rossiter ought to be concerned, no matter how much venom Drew Addison chooses to spill because he has been outshone at Dolly Dalingridge's ball! What can he do to harm him, after all?"

"Well, I don't know *that*," Lady Constance said with dignity, "because one never *does* know what foolish things gentlemen will take it into their heads to do, like old General Kincheloe when he thought his solicitor's clerk was cutting him out with a *most* unsuitable young female he had become entangled with—quite shocking at his age because he was all of seventy and his daughters, very respectable women, both of them, never dared hold up their heads in Society again—"

"Well—what *did* he do?" enquired Cressida, her curiosity piqued as Lady Constance, breaking off her sentence, sat meditating upon the scandalous past with a severe expression upon her face.

"I am sorry to say," said Lady Constance impressively, "that he attempted to horsewhip the young man in Bond Street when he was walking in company with the young woman, and the young woman wrested the horsewhip from him and beat the General instead. Of course," she added, "he—the General, I mean—withdrew all his business from the solicitor, which made him—the solicitor, that is—quite furious—"

But Cressida was no longer listening, owing to almost having the giggles in a very schoolgirlish way over the ridiculous tale, which somehow made her feel better about life in general. Or perhaps it was the news that the Honourable Drew Addision was also taking an interest of a sort in Kitty Chenevix that had accomplished that, for in spite of her disparagement of him she could not help feeling that he might be a far more solid obstacle than Captain Harries could ever be in preventing Rossiter from making a fool of himself over that very devious young female.

Not, she told herself, that Rossiter did not thoroughly deserve to have just such a wife, and she would certainly dance at their wedding if it ever came to that pass.

CHAPTER 7

In the days that followed, Cressida found she had every reason to believe in the possibility that she might indeed be required to fulfil her mentally expressed willingness to dance at the wedding of Rossiter and Kitty Chenevix. Certainly it could not be doubted that the Captain grasped every opportunity to be in company with Miss Chenevix: he called almost daily in Mount Street, took her driving in the Park behind his team of match-greys, and at every *ton* ball stood up with her for as many dances as Lady Constance's sense of propriety would allow.

Meanwhile, Captain Harries appeared to have dropped quite out of the running, though he too called frequently in Mount Street; but this, it was presumed by Lady Constance at least, was to see Cressida, not Kitty, and as a result it gave rise to a rather perturbed and disjointed conversation between her and Cressida, in which she said really, what would Langmere think of that young man's being so very often at the house, and Cressida said she did not care a rush what Langmere thought, or anyone else, either, and she would choose her friends as she pleased.

All of which made matters a trifle uncomfortable in the elegant house in Mount Street, and they were made still more so—for Cressida, at least—by the daily irritation of having to sit with her tongue between her teeth while Lady Constance went into raptures over Kitty's success, her character, and her manners. Such a *sweet* girl!—and did Cressida know that even Mrs. Drummond Burrell, the starchiest of the august Patronesses of Almack's, had commended her modest behaviour in the face of all the notoriety Rossiter's attentions had focussed upon her?

As for Addison, said Lady Constance, though he, too, was now making Kitty the object of his gallantry, there was certainly nothing to be hoped for in that direction, and so she, Lady Constance, had warned her; for Addison was a confirmed bachelor and prized his freedom far too highly to be caught in parson's mousetrap even by the most cleverly laid bait.

Still, there was no denying that he could be very charming when he chose, and that any young lady must think herself fortunate to attract his notice, as it must inevitably add to her consequence.

As for Kitty herself, she accepted her good fortune with a quiet composure that made Cressida wonder at times if she had already foreseen it when she had formed her plan of entering the world of the *haut ton* by way of the audacious deception she had practised.

"How *does* she do it?" she heard Dolly Dalingridge say at her elbow one evening at a crowded ball, just as she herself, watching Kitty as she danced with Rossiter, had been thinking precisely the same thing in her own mind. Dolly's rouged lips were pursed in an expression of contemptuous discontent: she had not yet got over her pique with Rossiter, and Kitty's success in attracting where she herself had failed had had the effect of adding Miss Chenevix to the list of her aversions. "Little Goody

Two Shoes and that—that *corsair!* Positively, it boggles the imagination! what *does* he see in her?"

"Peace. Calm. Domestic bliss," said Addison's voice behind her, urbanely intruding into the conversation. "No, don't say *Fustian* to me," he went on, as Dolly's lips made an impatient movement. "Obviously the corsair has tired of his *très mouvementé* life and now longs for the tranquillity of his own fireside. And you will allow, Dolly, that Miss Chenevix will make him a most conformable wife if he installs her as the chatelaine of the stately mansion he is even now searching for, it seems, if one is to believe Dame Rumour—who, as you know, is often so very tiresomely correct."

"Rossiter—searching for a house! Nonsense! You can't be serious!" Cressida exclaimed, startled by the unexpectedness of Addison's words into a betrayal of her surprise. "He is a bird of passage!"

"My dear, we all come to it in time," Addison said sententiously. "Slippers and a warm fire—" Cressida shrugged incredulously. "But for what other reason, my Cressy," persisted Addison, "could he be pursuing a milk-and-water miss and dreaming of a home in the country? He is not in love: her worst enemy would not accuse little Miss Chenevix of being capable of inspiring an overmastering passion in any man's breast—"

"Well, there you are mistaken, for she has," said Cressida decidedly.

"Who? Who?" clamoured Addison and Dolly in unison; but Cressida was not to be lured into revealing Captain Harries's secret and, turning the tables neatly upon Addison, said what about himself?

"I? My dear Cressy, that is spite, not love," said Addison placidly, flicking open an elegant Sèvres snuffbox with his left hand, *á la* Brummell, and taking a delicate pinch between thumb and forefinger. "It amuses me, you know, to see the all-conquering Captain chafing in a corner while his inamorata dances with me. As for little Miss Chenevix—I am living, I confess, in breathless expectation of seeing that sweet composure of hers melt one day into utter confusion as she endeavours to make up her mind between Rossiter and me."

"Yes, but *you* have no intention of marrying the girl," Dolly said, tapping his arm reprovingly with her fan. "You really are a dreadful beast, Drew. And the worst of it is that you are so disgracefully frank about your machinations. Aren't you afraid that Cressy will run straight home and tell Miss Chenevix all about your intentions—or had I best say, your lack of them? And *that* will put an end to your pretty little game."

"Not at all," said Addison, dusting an imaginary speck of snuff from his sleeve with an elegant gold-spotted muslin handkerchief of the style that had prompted the Prince Regent, in emulative envy, to order a dozen replicas at twelve guineas each. "Such a course of action would merely convince her that Cressy is jealous of my attentions to her—to say nothing of the fact," he added, looking reflectively at Cressida, "that I don't believe Cressy has the least intention of saying anything of the sort to her. A little jealousy in good earnest on your part, my love?"

"What—of you, or of Rossiter?" Cressida said lightly. "What vain creatures you men are, to be sure!"

"And yet, all the same, my dear, confess!—you don't care for the sweet, the demure, the almost too perfect Miss Chenevix."

"Nonsense! What has 'caring for her' to say to anything?" Cressida said, with an indifferent lift of her shoulders. "She is a very agreeable girl, and you could do far worse than to marry her. In point of fact, from what I know of you both, I think the two of you should deal extremely"—with which rather cryptic remark she rose and walked off, feeling that, if she remained, Addison, who had already come uncomfortably near the truth in one respect, might tell her something she did not wish to hear.

She did not feel it incumbent upon her to recount this conversation to Kitty when they had returned to Mount Street that night, but she did drop a hint to Lady Constance to the effect that Addison had been more than usually frank that evening as to his lack of any serious intentions towards the girl, knowing that Lady Constance would use the information to reinforce the warnings she had already given Kitty on the subject. For her own part, she felt that her thoughts were dwelling with quite ridiculous persistence upon the rumour Addison had imparted to her that Rossiter was looking for a country house—ridiculous, indeed, for of what possible interest could it be to her where he lived, or whether he had in truth made up his mind to settle himself and marry Kitty Chenevix?

And then on the following day something occurred that made her see that it was very much her affair, after all.

It began with a note brought to her by hand from Sir Octavius, requesting her to name a time at which it might be convenient for him to call upon her on a matter of urgent business. She was at that moment about to step into her barouche to purchase the latest volume of Sir Walter Scott's poems at Hatchard's and visit her milliner, who had signified that she had some new and ravishing creations to display to her; but, learning from the clerk who had brought the message that Sir Octavius would be free to see her if she were to go to his office at once, she altered her plans and instructed her coachman to drive to the City instead.

She found Sir Octavius in his austerely splendid office, and quite prepared, she soon discovered, to spend an unusually long period of time in social gossip before coming down to what had been presented to her as a matter of urgent business.

"What *are* you up to, Octavius?" she enquired presently in a rather suspicious tone. "And don't say *Nothing* because I know you too well to believe anything of the sort. You can't possibly be interested in how many times I stood up with Langmere at the Herrings' ball."

"Ah, but I am," said Sir Octavius tranquilly. "It will make rather a difference, you see, in how you receive my news if you are planning to marry him."

He looked at her quizzically, observing that her colour remained the same.

"Of course I am not planning on marrying him *now*," she said. "In point of fact, he hasn't asked me."

"Which tells me very little, you know," remarked Sir Octavius, "as tomorrow you may give me an exactly opposite answer with an equally good conscience. That is the worst thing about women: they change their minds."

"So do men," said Cressida, thinking unaccountably, and much to her annoyance, of a younger Rossiter who had asked her to marry him with every appearance of wishing her to do so, and then had apparently had second thoughts. "You had better tell me about it, whatever it is," she said to Sir Octavius. "And I really cannot see what difference it will make to anything whether I am to marry Langmere or not."

Sir Octavius, looking at her with his very expressive right eyebrow raised rather higher than usual, said perhaps, but it appeared to him that the Marchioness of Langmere, with estates in Sussex, Leicestershire, and Derbyshire, to say nothing of one of the most desirable town houses in London, might be rather less interested than might Miss Cressida Calverton in the fact that Calverton Place was about to be sold out of the family.

"Calverton Place?" Cressida stared at him. "What on earth are you talking of, Octavius? Do you mean to tell me that Uncle Arthur is thinking of selling it? But he can't be. It is entailed."

"Mr. Walter Calverton, the heir, has agreed to break the entail, I believe," Sir Octavius said. And, as Cressida still looked unconvinced, "My dear girl, it is quite the soundest thing that he could do," he went on. "You must be aware that your uncle has already sold all the land it was possible for him to sell, and that there is very little left besides the house itself and the gardens and park—all of which are heavily mortgaged. As matters are arranged at the present time, Mr. Walter Calverton stands to inherit a mountain of debt and a house he cannot afford to live in, which is fast falling into ruin because of neglect. And as he is a very distant relation of your uncle's—is he not?"

Cressida nodded.

"—and can have no sentimental attachment to the place," Sir Octavius continued, "it would certainly appear wiser for him to arrange matters with your uncle now in such a way that he—that is, your uncle—will be able to accept the very advantageous offer he has received."

"An advantageous offer? For Calverton Place? But who can wish to buy it?" Cressida demanded. "I haven't seen the house for years, but it was falling to rack even then."

"I believe," said Sir Octavius, looking at the tips of his fingers, which he had joined together in a very legalistic way, though with his eyebrow still quizzically raised, "that the prospective purchaser is a gentleman named Rossiter. To be precise, Captain Deverell Rossiter—"

If he had anticipated a lively reaction to his words, he was not disappointed. Cressida said, "Rossiter!" in an incredulous tone, and then, "*Rossiter!*" again, with indignation now uppermost, after which she rose and began to pace up and down the room, looking so very handsome in her anger that Sir Octavius regretted all over again that he was not twenty years younger and precluded by his business interests from falling in love. "This," she said presently, pausing and gazing at him with a martial light in her eyes, "is insupportable!"

"No, is it?" Sir Octavius looked at her blandly. "I confess I really don't quite see why."

"He is doing it on purpose!" Cressida said accusingly.

"Well, yes," acknowledged Sir Octavius. "A man usually does not buy an estate, I believe, unless it is *on purpose,* as you say."

"I mean on purpose to be disagreeable to me!" Cressida said inexorably. "There must be dozens of other houses he could buy! *Hundreds* of them! And he doesn't even care for Gloucestershire! He told me so once."

"Perhaps," said Sir Octavius, with a deceptively innocent air, "he has changed his mind."

Cressida gave him an indignant glance and resumed her pacing.

"Well, I won't have it!" she declared presently. "If anyone has the right to buy Calverton Place, it is me—*I*! And why Uncle Arthur was tottyheaded enough not to apply to *me* when he found himself at Point Non-Plus, instead of going about to sell the estate to a perfect stranger—"

Sir Octavius shook his head. "Well, I won't say it wouldn't have been better if he had done so," he agreed judicially. "But Mr. Arthur Calverton—if you will forgive my saying so, my dear—has never been distinguished by the possession of even a moderate amount of common sense. And no doubt he felt a certain embarrassment in revealing to you into how desperate a state he had allowed his affairs to fall."

"Well, he is going to feel even more embarrassed when I tell him what I think of this—this nonsensical scheme of his!" Cressida declared. "Which, of course, he will *not* be allowed to go through with! I shall go to Gloucestershire myself at once."

"But I rather fancy you are too late, my child," said Sir Octavius, who was looking somewhat amused by the tempest his disclosure had aroused, but at the same time was regarding Cressida with an even more keenly penetrating gaze than usual, as if he found something very revealing in her wrath. "According to the information I have received, matters have already gone so far that any attempt at interference on your part at this time will probably be quite unavailing."

"Nonsense!" said Cressida impatiently. "If documents have been signed, they must—they must just *un*sign them, or tear them up, or whatever must be done to make them of no effect! It is all a great piece of absurdity! Naturally, as a Calverton, *I* must have Calverton Place!"

"But you have never shown the smallest interest in it before this time," Sir Octavius reminded her, looking still more amused. "How was your uncle to have known you would feel this way? No, no, Cressy, it won't do!" he went on, as she turned to him, about to make some wrathful reply. "You have accused Rossiter of wishing to buy Calverton Place only to spite you, but are you quite sure that the shoe is not on the other foot, and that *you* are determined he shall not have it only in order to spite *him*?"

A flush came up in Cressida's face. "That," she said, achieving with some difficulty a dignified tone, "is *quite* unworthy of you, Octavius!"

"On the contrary, my dear, it is quite unworthy of *you*, if it is true. It's not like you to bear malice—"

"I am *not* bearing malice! It is only that—that I

don't want him to have Calverton Place!" Cressida said, with a sudden rather horrid feeling that Sir Octavius was quite right, and that if it had been anyone but Rossiter who wished to buy Calverton Place she would not have been nearly so angry about it.

Unfortunately, as is the case with most people, knowing that she was in the wrong did not make her any more reconciled to the situation, and when she took her leave of Sir Octavius shortly afterwards she was still quite unregenerate in her resolution to go to Gloucestershire at once and see what could be done in the matter of wresting Calverton Place from Rossiter's grasp.

It did occur to her to wonder, as she was driving back to Mount Steet, why Sir Octavius had made such a point of seeing to it that she was made aware of Rossiter's intention to purchase it, particularly as he appeared to feel that any interference in the transaction on her part would be not only ill-judged but unavailing as well. But she had no time to go into that matter now, her mind being entirely preoccupied with plans for arranging a journey to Calverton Place at the earliest possible moment.

On arriving back in Mount Street, she had the intention of putting those plans into effect at once by ordering her travelling-chaise to be made ready, instructing Moodle to pack up a suitable selection of clothes and other necessaries for the journey, and despatching an army of messengers to carry her excuses for all the social events to which she had accepted invitations for the next several days. But to her annoyance she was met at the front door by Harbage, with the news that Lord Langmere had called to see her a few minutes before and was awaiting her return in the drawing room.

"Bother!" she exclaimed under her breath, and walked into the drawing room at once, where she found Lord Langmere looking through a copy of one of Mr.

Southey's recent poems, *The Curse of Kehama,* with an expression of entirely lukewarm interest upon his face.

"Well, Leonard? What is it?" she enquired, dispensing with formal greetings as she came forward towards him across the floor.

He rose, putting the book aside, and with the expression of slight surprise that had appeared upon his face at the sound of her rather impatient tone deepening as he took in her heightened colour.

"Is anything amiss?" he countered. "You seem disturbed—"

"Well, I am!" Cressida admitted frankly, stripping off her gloves and flinging herself into a chair. "Would you believe it, Leonard?—that odious Rossiter is arranging to buy Calverton Place from my uncle! The entail is to be broken—I daresay you are not acquainted with my cousin, Walter Calverton, who is the heir, but he is as improvident a creature as Uncle Arthur, whom you *do* know, and far more feckless—and Rossiter, of all men, is bargaining to buy the place! Of course I shall not allow it. I am going to Gloucestershire at once to put matters to rights."

"To Gloucestershire?" Lord Langmere sat down again, looking slightly staggered by this sudden announcement. "But, my dear Cressy, in the middle of the Season—is this really necessary?" he asked. "Surely your solicitors can handle the matter."

"My solicitors," said Cressida, "cannot handle Uncle Arthur. I can. This will not do, you know, Leonard—Rossiter to have Calverton Place! It is quite unthinkable! If Uncle Arthur has come to any sort of agreement with him, it will simply have to be set aside."

Lord Langmere, perceiving by these words that there was more to the matter than had at first appeared, began to look serious.

"*Has* an agreement been reached between them?"

he asked. "If that is the case, I fear there is very little that you can do—that is, if Captain Rossiter wishes to hold your uncle to the bargain."

"I can offer him a good deal more than he has paid for the property himself," Cressida retorted. "*That* would do the trick with most men. Whether it will with Rossiter remains to be seen. But he shan't have Calverton Place! I shall see to that, if it takes half my fortune!"

Lord Langmere was looking increasingly surprised by her vehemence. "But surely it can't mean so much to you," he said. "You have never appeared to interest yourself—"

"Very well, then—I haven't! But I never imagined before this time that Uncle Arthur would think of selling the estate—and to Rossiter, of all men!" She stood up abruptly. "I am sorry, Leonard, but I really *must* have things made ready for the journey," she said. "You didn't wish to see me for any particular reason—did you?"

Lord Langmere, suddenly looking rather rueful, said that as a matter of fact, he did.

"Oh?" Cressida looked questioning. "The Boltons' evening-party? But I shan't be able to attend, of course."

"*Not* the Boltons' evening-party." Lord Langmere's expression became still more rueful. "I am quite aware that this is not the propitious time to ask you," he said, "but I had screwed up my courage to the sticking-point, you see, and I don't know when I shall be able to do it again. Cressy, my dear, *will* you marry me and forget all about Gloucestershire and Calverton Place and everything else that threatens to separate us even for the space of four-and-twenty hours?"

Cressida, with the sensation of being in the sort of dream in which all sorts of important, frightening, and triumphant things happen to one at the most vexingly unsuitable moments, felt both her hands being taken in an urgent masculine grasp, and only by exercising great presence of mind did she manage to avoid being enveloped in a full embrace.

"Leonard—no!" she said, quickly stepping back a pace. "At least, I don't mean *no*, exactly, but—but you are quite right: this is *not* the time," she went on, astonished to find herself speaking almost as incoherently as a girl in her first Season receiving her first offer. "You have taken me quite by surprise—"

If Lord Langmere had been capable upon his own side of speaking sensibly, he would have told her that any young woman who, having received the extremely marked attentions he had lavished upon her over a period of several months, professed surprise over their culminating in an offer of marriage was being either idiotish or intolerably missish. Not being capable of such rational thinking, however, he merely found her confusion captivating and attempted again, this time more successfully, to take her in his arms.

"Oh, *dear!*" said Cressida. "Really, Leonard, you mustn't! I must have time to think!"

"You have had quite enough already," said Lord Langmere firmly. "You must have known how I feel about you—"

But by this time Cressida, calling upon the reserves of experience gained in half a dozen years of dealing with importunate suitors, had matters well in hand again, and said with equal firmness that she hadn't.

"Had enough time, that is," she said. "You *can't* ask someone to marry you when she is on her way to Gloucestershire and expect her to give you a sensible answer."

"But you needn't be on your way to Gloucestershire," Lord Langmere protested, making another attempt to embrace his love and finding himself, he was never to know exactly how, standing quite alone in the middle of the floor while his love made some slight alterations to her coiffure in the mirror above the green jasperware Wedgwood fireplace.

All very cool and Londonish, his lordship, who considered himself to be genuinely in love, albeit somewhat past the age of violent romantic fancies, thought bitterly. But that was Cressida, who was well known never to give any of her suitors the satisfaction of putting off her elusive ways and standing still to be properly kissed.

As for Cressida herself, she went upstairs, having dismissed Lord Langmere very kindly with a promise to let him know his fate the moment she returned from Gloucestershire, and for all of five minutes was very cross with herself for having been so ridiculously missish as not to have given his lordship a plain, round answer and thus put them both out of their misery.

Now, she thought, she would have to worry herself all the way to Calverton Place and during her negotiations there with her uncle as to whether she should or shouldn't; but to say the truth, in the bustle of her preparations for her journey she had forgotten all about poor Lord Langmere within a quarter of an hour, and did not think of him again until she was getting into bed that night in the very comfortable bedchamber of the Oxford inn where she broke her journey—which, if his lordship had known of it, he might or might not have considered a propitious omen.

CHAPTER 8

Having spurred her postillions on to their best efforts from the time she left Oxford, Cressida was able to arrive at Calverton Place well before the dinner hour on the following day.

It had been several years since she had been in the Cotswold country, and the sight of honey-coloured stone houses with moss-covered slate roofs set beside little streams spanned by miniature bridges, of lanes decked in the pink and gold of lady's smock and cowslips, and of the long, sweet green-grey sweep of the high wold rippling off into the distance, filled her with an exhilarating and nostalgic sense of being very young again, the green girl who had freely wandered these hills and woods, and who had come with mingled trepidation and anticipation to Cheltenham's neat terraces and stucco villas. London fell from her as if it had been no more than the elegantly fashionable redingote of slate-coloured twilled sarsnet she was wearing, and by the time her chaise turned in at the gates of Calverton Place she would not have been surprised to look down and see it replaced by a school-girl's plain round kerseymere frock, defaced by bramble tears and berry stains from a day's ramble in the woods.

Calverton Place was a classical seventeenth-century mansion built of pale gold limestone and set across the bottom of a deep, tree-planted valley, with hills rising behind it. There was a recessed central block with shallow projections at each end, and a pillared entrance over which the Calverton eagle spread enormous wings from the pediment above. Even when Cressida first remembered it, the park had been overgrown and the gardens neglected, but it had been going gently from bad to worse ever since, until now it had rather the look, she thought, of having done it on purpose, like the impenetrable thicket that had sprung up to protect the Sleeping Beauty's slumber in the fairy tale.

The house, too, when she reached it and alighted from her chaise, had the same rather delightfully melancholy air of having been deserted by humanity for countless centuries—an effect that was somewhat spoiled by the appearance, in response to her knock, of an incongruously young and fresh-faced butler whom she had never seen before, and who stared in obvious surprise at her travelling-chaise, from which Moodle was in the act of extracting her dressing-case, while one of the postillions dealt with the other luggage.

"No, I'm not expected," Cressida said cheerfully, in answer to the butler's mutely questioning face. "Is my uncle in? I am Miss Calverton."

The butler, standing aside for her to enter the hall, said he regretted that Mr. Calverton was not in, but that it was certain he would return soon, being only gone out to show the gentleman about the park.

"The gentleman? You *don't* mean—you *can't* mean —Captain Rossiter?" asked Cressida, slightly taken aback.

"Yes, miss," said the butler, and looked a trifle nervously at Moodle, who had followed Cressida into the house and was gazing about in grim disapproval at the hall, which had had all its good pieces sold—and what was left, her accusing eyes told him, was sadly in need of polishing. "May I ask, miss," he enquired, once more addressing Cressida, "if—if you are expecting to stay—"

"Well, it does make it a bit awkward that my uncle is not here to ask me, but I am," Cressida said frankly. "Perhaps I might have the Blue Bedchamber—"

The butler, looking even more nervously at Moodle, who was now radiating scorn over his lack of "manner," said he was afraid Captain Rossiter was occupying the Blue Bedchamber at present.

"What—is he *staying* here?" Cressida exclaimed, a trifle indignantly. "Oh, very well, then—the Green."

The butler's fresh-coloured face grew even pinker and he stammered, with an apprehensive glance at Moodle, that he was very sorry indeed, but the Green Bedchamber, too, was occupied.

"By a Lady," he amplified his statement, so obviously capitalising the word that Cressida immediately understood that a lady of title was involved.

"Oh?" she said, intrigued, wondering what odd sort of party her uncle had got up for Rossiter, or if "the Lady" had perhaps come with Rossiter himself. "A Lady?"

"Yes, miss. Lady Letitia Conway," said the butler, which startled Cressida so much that she exclaimed involuntarily, "Good God, what is *she* doing here?"

For Lady Letitia was an elderly cousin of Arthur Calverton's who resided in Cheltenham, went in largely for charitable works, being unmarried and with a great deal of time on her hands, and was considered by her cousin Arthur an infernal bore.

The butler, apparently feeling that answering Cressida's question was above and beyond the call of duty, said he couldn't take it upon himself to say, but added helpfully that she had arrived the evening before. He kept to himself the interesting fact that Lady Letitia, too, had obviously not been expected, and that a quarrel of titanic proportions had taken place between her and her host in the library that morning, of which he had unfortunately been able to overhear only the less interesting portions consisting of his employer's rejoinders, since Lady Letitia, being a "Lady" in every sense of the word, never raised her voice, and would no doubt, if called upon to do so, have pronounced even the dread ecclesiastical curse of Anathema Maranatha in the mild, confidential tones suitable for a drawing-room tête-à-tête.

But this piece of information would have been lost upon Cressida even if he had volunteered it, for, having ascertained that Lady Letitia was at that moment in the library, she went off at once in that direction.

The library at Calverton Place was a large square apartment hung with gilded leather, now sadly darkened by time, and with a fine plaster ceiling typical of its period, boasting a central oval wreath of tightly packed foliage and flowers. Two striking torchères in the form of undraped nymphs balancing scallop shells on their heads flanked the Italian marble fireplace, and sitting bolt upright beside one of them, in an attitude of resigned disapproval that might have been evoked by their shameless proximity, or might, on the other hand, have arisen out of the apparently disagreeable thoughts that were occupying her at the moment, was Lady Letitia Conway. She was an excessively thin female with a long, mildly melancholy face, dressed in a shapeless and unfashionable frock of some grey material and with her grey hair untidily arranged upon the top of her head.

Her face lightened immediately, however, at sight of Cressida, whose quite unexpected appearance at Calverton Place did not seem to occasion the least surprise to her.

"Cressida, *darling*," she said in her almost inaudible voice, as she rose to embrace her. "So *good* of you to come. And so *soon*. I had scarcely dared to hope—it is such a *long* way from London. But now you are here, we must put our heads together at once. Such a *terrible* thing to be thinking of doing—" She put her head on one side, regarding Cressida's surprised face interrogatively. "I am sure you must agree with me?"

"If you mean Uncle Arthur's thinking of selling Calverton Place, I agree entirely," Cressida said, tossing her elegant bonnet upon a table and seating herself. "But how *could* you have known I was coming, Cousin Letty? You simply couldn't have done: I didn't know it myself until a few hours before I left London."

"Oh," said Lady Letitia, looking astonished, "then you *didn't* get my letter? But there—of course you didn't!" She peered into her reticule, which was made of papier-maché in the form of an Etruscan vase, in a style that had been fashionable in France during the Directoire, and produced with an air of triumph a sealed missive, which she held up for Cressida to see. "I only wrote it this morning and I haven't posted it yet," she said. "But I *did* ask you most earnestly in it to come, and of course I imagined—" She lowered her voice to a still more inaudible whisper. "Naturally I came at once myself, as soon as I heard what he was planning to do," she said. "I considered it my duty to Speak to Him; nothing, as I told him *most* emphatically this morning, will induce me to countenance his selling Calverton Place out of the family. Not," she added, looking at Cressida with imploring eyes and a slight flush in her thin cheeks, "that there is anything that I can do to prevent it. Arthur is really most unaccountably obstinate. But I am sure that *you*, dearest Cressida—"

"Well, I shall certainly do my best," said Cressida, but feeling somehow that Lady Letitia's having got in before her with Arthur Calverton put her at a disadvantage. People—especially people like her uncle Arthur, who liked things to arrange themselves without any undue fuss or trouble—had the disagreeable habit of digging in their heels and laying back their ears when opposition threatened to disturb a comfortable *status quo,* and the fact that Lady Letitia's well-meant meddling had apparently already caused this process to set in would, Cressida considered, most assuredly not make her task any the easier.

But she had no opportunity to reflect on what alteration in her tactics this unexpected change in the situation ought to bring about when her uncle himself, followed by Rossiter, walked into the room.

Arthur Calverton was a small, dapper man with greying hair and a nice taste in waistcoats, who had a genius for backing slow horses and a penchant for quiet little games of whist for large stakes, from which he hardly ever seemed to rise a winner. Cressida had held him in somewhat exasperated affection all her life, but felt the exasperation rather getting the upper hand of the affection now as she saw the alarmed roll of the eyes with which he took in her unexpected presence in his library.

"Cressy, my dear! Didn't expect to see *you* in these parts just now—middle of the Season and all that!" he said, assuming a quite transparently false air of welcoming jollity as he advanced to fold her in a brief embrace and give her an unenthusiastic peck upon the cheek. "Nothing wrong in town—eh?"

"Nothing at all," said Cressida coolly; and, deciding to take the bull by the horns, she went on at once, "I've come because I heard you are thinking of selling Calverton Place."

"Selling Calverton Place?" For a moment it seemed that Arthur Calverton might have intended taking craven refuge in a denial, but, with Rossiter standing politely silent behind him, instant realisation of the futility of such a course obviously overcame him, and he said hastily, in what was apparently intended as an off-hand manner, "Best thing to do under the circumstances, my dear. Dashed millstone around the neck and all that for these past few years—place falling to rack—feller'd need the brass of a nabob to keep it up. And Walter's agreeable—says he'll be glad to be rid of the place—" He broke off, looking around rather guiltily at Rossiter. "You two *do* know each other, don't you?" he asked. "Seem to remember—"

"We were engaged once, Uncle Arthur," Cressida said, looking at Rossiter with an expression that plainly told him she had said it only to deny him the pleasure of saying it himself.

But instead of acknowledging that he had been checkmated, he only grinned at her.

"A chapter in your life that you would prefer to forget, Cressy?" he drawled. "No—don't answer that: I am full of kindly feelings towards all Calvertons today, and I shouldn't be able to put my heart into a quarrel with one of them." He strolled across the room and sat down opposite her, and again she felt, as she had done more than once since they had renewed their acquaintance at the start of the Season, the mocking, reckless intensity of his gaze upon her, as if he were endeavouring to strip the veneer of London sophistication from her and penetrate to the real person beneath.

This, of course, always made her quite determined that he should do nothing of the sort, and as a result she assumed her most Londonish air and said that she, too, hoped they were not to quarrel.

"You have only to tell me that you quite see the unsuitability of anyone outside the family buying Calverton Place, and I assure you I shall be the soul of amiability," she said airily; and was not at all surprised to see his black brows snap together in a sudden frown.

"Have I, by God?" he said, thus causing Lady Letitia to open her faded, anxious blue eyes very wide and say something in a reproachful voice, but fortunately so inaudibly that no one understood it. "So that is why you are here," continued the Captain rather grimly—"to thrust a spoke in my wheel. Well, it won't do, Cressy— not even if you are prepared to buy Calverton Place yourself—"

"It is exactly what I am prepared to do," said Cressida, in such a calm, well-bred, and altogether condescending tone that anyone would have forgiven Captain Rossiter the desire to beat her that was for a moment expressed quite clearly upon his dark face. "And what is more," she continued, "it is what I intend to do."

Arthur Calverton, scenting battle in the air, hastily rang for his butler and said they would all have some sherry.

"Not for me, Arthur dear," said Lady Letitia, looking shocked. "And I should think not for you, either, just at this time. We are talking business, and I remember dear Papa's always saying, Sherry *after* business, because one needed a clear head—"

Arthur Calverton said rather crossly that they weren't talking business as far as he could see, and if she meant the house, that was all settled now.

"We'll have the Oloroso," he said to the butler, who had by this time appeared in the doorway. He turned to Rossiter. "*Not* the best year," he said. "The bloodsuckers got all that. Sold up to pay a tailor's bill, if you'll believe it. Enough to make a grown man cry."

Rossiter, who appeared to have lost interest quickly in the sudden crossing of swords between himself and Cressida that had alarmed their host, said that he had observed the depleted state of the cellars, and that when he came to restocking them he would be glad of Mr. Calverton's expert advice. This statement quite soothed Mr. Calverton, and set him off on a learned monologue on the comparative merits of Oloroso and Manzanilla, and the difficulty nowadays in obtaining the good Mountain-Malaga one had been able to procure in his youth—all of which left Cressida stranded high and dry on the rocks of her own indignation and certainly got her no further in her intention of thwarting the projected sale of Calverton Place to Rossiter.

She was not in the least daunted in her determination to carry out this intention, however, and, taking advantage of the momentary preoccupation of the gentlemen with their talk of wine, moved to seat herself beside Lady Letitia and say to her in a low voice, "It will do no good to say any more of the matter now, with Rossiter in the room. I shall contrive to see Uncle Arthur alone a little later."

"Yes, *do*, my dear!" Lady Letitia whispered fervently. "He does not listen to me, you know; he never has. I remember very clearly that when we were both quite small children—"

But the arrival of the butler with the sherry interrupted the no doubt interesting reminiscences in which Lady Letitia was about to indulge, and Cressida, seizing the opportunity to escape, pleaded the fatigue of her journey and went upstairs to the bedchamber that had been prepared for her.

CHAPTER 9

Cressida lost no time in contriving a private conversation with her uncle. There was, indeed, little difficulty in managing it, for the door of her bedchamber was exactly opposite the door of his, and she had only to leave it ajar a trifle while they were both dressing for dinner, and when she heard him come out follow him down the stairs and herd him, though much against his will, into the little sitting room off the half-landing.

"I want to talk to you, Uncle," she said, at which ominous words Mr. Calverton nearly bolted, but was restrained by the fact that she was standing in the doorway.

To an unbiassed observer, Cressida, in the gown she had chosen to wear that evening—an underdress of sea-green silk veiled by a tunic of paler green gossamer-thin muslin—would have seemed a charming figure as she stood there; but to Mr. Calverton, filled with guilty consciousness of his own shortcomings, she had more the appearance of an avenging Nemesis.

"Yes, my dear," he said hastily. "Certainly! But not at this moment. My guests, you know—Letty, Captain

Rossiter—afraid they don't quite get on with each other. Wouldn't do to leave them alone together—"

"Cousin Letty hasn't come down yet, and you will be able to hear her when she does," Nemesis said ruthlessly, and then made matters worse by coming over and slipping an arm coaxingly through his. "Do let us sit down here together for just a moment, Uncle," she said.

Mr. Calverton, finding that his reluctant feet were being guided irresistibly to a horridly uncomfortable cane-backed settee, which only lived there now because the Hepplewhite sofa that had used to stand in its place had been sold, sat down and fidgeted.

"And don't fidget, darling," said Cressida soothingly. "There really is not the slightest need, you know. You have only to sell Calverton Place to me instead of to Rossiter, and everything will be *quite* comfortable. How much has he offered you for it? I am prepared to go a full thousand higher."

Mr. Calverton looked at her unhappily. He had really not the slightest objection to selling his ancestral estate to his niece, and the lure of an extra thousand pounds to a gentleman who perennially found himself, as he expressed it, without a feather to fly with, was not inconsiderable. Unfortunately, his situation at the present time was such that, no matter how his own inclinations stood, he was unable to take advantage of Cressida's offer, and so he regretfully informed her.

"Papers already drawn up and signed with Rossiter, m'dear," he said. "Couldn't get out of the bargain if I wanted to. Pity, because if I'd known you were interested in buying the place, of course I'd have been happy to let you have it."

"You *would* have known," Cressida said in pardonable reproach, "if you had given me the least inkling you were thinking of doing such a thing. Really, Uncle, you *have* managed the affair very badly, you know!"

"Well, how was I to guess you'd take it into your head to want to buy a ramshackle old place like this?" Mr. Calverton retorted, stung into defending himself by this frontal attack. "From all I've heard of your doings lately, you're on the verge of getting yourself riveted to Langmere, and the Lord knows *he* has no need for another house!"

Cressida said with dignity that people who listened to gossip were unfortunately very often deceived.

"You mean you're *not* going to marry him?" Mr. Calverton said incredulously. "The biggest catch of the Season, and you're going to whistle him down the wind? You must be all about in your head, my girl!"

"No, I am not!" said Cressida, nettled. "I haven't said I shan't marry him; I simply haven't made up my mind as yet."

"Well, you'd best make it up soon, then," Mr. Calverton advised her, with a masculine lack of tact. "A man like Langmere ain't going to stay dangling at your shoestrings forever, you know. Too many other females on the catch for him." And he went on, with sudden inspiration, "If you don't care to have *him*, why don't you marry Rossiter? Engaged to him once, you say—must have thought it was a good idea then. *That* would settle the matter nicely; then you could both have Calverton Place."

Cressida, giving him a speaking look, said she had never heard a more addlepated suggestion, as she would not marry Rossiter for a hundred Calverton Places and she was sure he himself had other plans.

"No, has he?" said Mr. Calverton, looking interested. "I rather wondered about that, you know—I mean, buying this place and all that. Who is she? Anyone I know?"

"No," said Cressida, and then was angry with herself for that momentary and unaccountable little act of cowardice, for why in heaven's name, she asked herself, could she not have said in plain words that it was generally believed in London that Rossiter was on the point of offering for Kitty Chenevix? "But all this has nothing to say to the matter," she hurried on. "What is important is that you really must tell Rossiter that you have decided you don't wish to sell, after all—"

"But I can't do that!" said Mr. Calverton, quite aghast at the impropriety of such an idea. "Good God, girl, no one but a woman would think of such a thing. And Octavius Mayr says you have a head for business!"

"I have—quite as good a one as yours, I daresay!" said Cressida defensively. "But I can't see why, when everyone *knows* you would have sold Calverton Place to me, instead of to Rossiter, if you had had the least idea I was prepared to buy it—"

"No!" said Mr. Calverton, with unexpected firmness. He got up and stood looking at her with an expression of alarmed resolution on his face. "Now, look here, Cressy," he said, "I'm dashed if I'm going to be hunted by a pair of women in my own house over a matter neither of 'em has the least right to meddle in! I've already had Letty ringing a peal over me about it, and I don't want another from you! Now you're welcome to stay here as long as you like—no, come to think of it, it's Rossiter's house now, but I daresay he won't object—but only if you'll agree to stop badgering me over something *I* can't do anything about—"

Fortunately for the maintenance of good relations between them, they were interrupted at this point by the sound of Lady Letitia's footsteps cautiously proceeding down the stairs.

"There's Letty," said Mr. Calverton hastily, and bolted, leaving Cressida to make up her mind in some vexation that the only course now left open to her was to approach Rossiter himself on the matter. Perhaps, she thought, if she was very civil to him and represented to him in a quiet and logical manner the impropriety of her uncle's having disposed of a property that had been in the family since the time of Charles I, he would see reason.

But she could not feel very sanguine in this hope. It was far more likely, she considered, that he would be his usual mocking, unco-operative self and that she would lose her temper. As for offering him a considerably higher sum for the house than he had paid for it, she did not think it would serve any good purpose since he had become so odiously rich, but she was prepared, as a last resort, to try this tack as well.

At dinner, which, owing to Lady Letitia's disapproving silence and Cressida's feeling of grievance against both Rossiter and her uncle, was not a very comfortable meal, she perfected her plans for her attack upon him. He and Mr. Calverton would, of course, remain in the dining room over their wine after she and Lady Letitia had retired to the Blue Saloon, but when the gentlemen joined them again she must, she thought, contrive a way to have Rossiter to herself, if only for a short time.

A less dashing and experienced young lady might have been hard put to it to find a way to bring this about in such a small party, but Cressida had not gained her reputation for taking the most direct means to an end, regardless of convention, for nothing, and when Rossiter appeared with her uncle in the Blue Saloon and strolled over to her chair she said to him at once, in a composed voice, "It is an intolerably warm evening to remain indoors—don't you agree? Shall we take a turn in the garden? You may smoke an after-dinner cheroot there without offending Cousin Letty—I daresay you *have* taken up that habit, like all the other men I know who served in the Peninsula?"

Any other gentleman of her acquaintance—with the possible exception of Addison, who considered that his pretensions to the role of *premier dandy* precluded him from exhibiting any emotion other than boredom—would have accepted this invitation with grateful alacrity; but Rossiter merely gazed down at her with what she felt was a rather sardonically amused expression on his dark face.

"So you haven't given up yet," he remarked. "I will say that for you, Cressy—you go down fighting to the last ditch. But it won't do you the least bit of good, you know. I'm quite immune to your charms, my dear, being well aware that any exhibition of them for my benefit has nothing but the coolest calculation behind it."

It was on the tip of Cressida's tongue to return a crushing rejoinder, but she had determined not to allow him to make her lose her temper, and, swallowing her wrath with some difficulty, she gave him an agreeable smile instead.

"Come, Dev," she said, "you have said yourself that it is folly for us to be at dagger-drawing with each other every time we meet. I *do* want Calverton Place from you—I admit it freely—but I am also stifling in this warm room, and of course Cousin Letty will raise an outcry if I suggest we have the windows opened. Why *do* people persist in sitting in tightly closed rooms even on the sultriest night?"

She rose as she spoke and, placing her hand on his arm, stood looking up at him, prepared for him to accompany her outside. He grinned and shrugged.

"Very well," he agreed. "Far be it from me to resist the opportunity for a tête-à-tête with the dashing Miss Calverton. But I warn you in advance, my girl, that you are going to all this trouble for nothing. I have got Calverton Place and I mean to keep it, no matter how inclined you are to play dog in the manger in the affair."

Once again Cressida swallowed the stinging retort

that rose to her lips, and, with an easy word to her uncle, who had sat down warily beside Lady Letitia, evidently considering her as the lesser of two evils, she walked out of the room beside Rossiter.

The Italian garden upon which an eighteenth-century Calverton had lavished a great deal of expense and irritation (having a Scottish gardener at the time who stubbornly resisted all foreign influences) had long since succumbed to the far more potent opposition of Nature: its once-neat box hedges were fantastically overgrown, and a riotous tangle of weeds of every variety known to the countryside reached out to brush the silken skirts of Cressida's gown as she and Rossiter strolled slowly along the paths.

"What a dreadful place this is!" she said on a determinedly light note, as she saw that Rossiter had obviously no intention of helping her out by beginning the conversation himself. "I can't think what can have made you consider buying such a ramshackle piece of property! It will obviously require a fortune to set it to rights."

"Yes, I rather think it will," Rossiter agreed imperturbably. "But I am quite prepared for that, you know. I shall have an army of workmen in here by next month, and I daresay the place will be presentable by autumn, though of course one can't make gardens in a day."

He had paused to look critically at a moss-covered stone satyr leaning aslant the path, its wickedly grinning face appearing even more eerie than its creator had probably intended it to be in the first faint starshine of the evening. Cressida, ignoring the satyr and concentrating on the living man, who was even more hateful to her at the moment, said hadn't he the least intention, then, of even listening to her reasons for wishing him to give up Calverton Place?

"No," said Rossiter baldly. His black eyes left the satyr and raked her with their uncomfortably penetrating gaze, which the slight, mocking smile curving his lips did little to make more agreeable to her. "My dear good girl, you may leave off smiling so complaisantly and speaking to me in those dulcet tones," he said. "I'm quite aware you would like to scratch my eyes out, in spite of all this show of amiability—but I can assure you that neither cajolery nor rage will get you Calverton Place. You cannot advance a single reason why I should give it up to you, beyond your dislike of seeing me have it—"

"Oh, what a *detestable* man you are!" Cressida exclaimed, her indignation surfacing at this piece of plain speaking, in spite of her resolution to remain calm. "I have the very best of reasons: *I* am a Calverton, and you are not!"

"Come—that's more like it!" Rossiter said, looking appreciatively at her wrathfully sparkling eyes. "I thought we should come to an end of all that amiability before long."

"And no wonder!" said Cressida fulminatingly. "You would try anyone's patience with that odiously cynical tongue of yours! I have been making every effort to be civil to you—"

"For purely selfish reasons, my girl; don't forget that," said Rossiter, quite unmoved by these self-justifying words.

He flicked the moss-grown satyr with a proprietary finger, and it promptly tottered and fell across the path, where it lay glaring balefully up at them.

"*Now* see what you have done!" said Cressida, becoming on the instant the outraged landowner. "I daresay it is broken—and an extremely valuable piece!"

"I'll make you a present of it," Rossiter said obligingly. "And if it wants repairing, you can send the bill to me."

"What on earth would I do with it?" Cressida asked

witheringly, and Rossiter replied at once that he expected Langmere had an Italian garden at each of his country seats, and she could decide after she had married him which it would best suit.

"And who told you, pray, that I am to marry Lord Langmere?" Cressida enquired, with considerable hauteur.

"What—aren't you? Don't tell me you are merely having one of your Maygames with that poor devil as well," Rossiter said bluntly. "You had best break yourself of that habit, Cressy; to say nothing of its not being a pretty one, you will find yourself lurched in the end. Even your fortune won't bring you a man worth having if you go on in *this* path. It's not agreeable to be made a fool of before the world, you know. Langmere has my sympathy—"

By the time he had got this far Cressida was so furious that she could scarcely speak.

"*Oh!*" she gasped. "I wish I were a man, so I could call you out, Dev Rossiter! How *dare* you—*you!*—speak to me so? I didn't jilt *you*—"

"No, my dear, as I understand *that* little affair, it was a matter of mutual agreement," Rossiter said smoothly. His dark eyes wore an expression that was quite unreadable in the faint starshine. "But you were young and green then, and hadn't yet discovered how amusing it can be to play a man like a fish on a line, and then cut him loose when you have tired of the game. But there is one thing," he went on, his voice taking on a suddenly sterner note under the jeering lightness with which he had previously spoken, "that I should warn you of. Don't think to add Miles Harries to the list of your victims or you'll have me to deal with. He's not one of your tonnish *cicisbeos* who knows the game as well as you do and can play it with as little heart."

He paused, and Cressida said, with awful calm,

"Have you *quite* finished?"

"I think so," said Rossiter coolly. He took a case from his pocket and extracted a Spanish cigar from it. "I daresay *you* haven't, but I should advise you in advance to save your breath. Telling me how much you dislike me may relieve your feelings, but the worst bear-garden jaw you can give me won't change my mind. May I suggest that you join your uncle and Lady Letitia instead? You and she may entertain each other by abusing me to your hearts' content, and I shall be able to blow a cloud in peace."

"Yes, I daresay you wish me to go away!" Cressida said, feeling how hot her cheeks were in the darkness and wondering, even in her indignation, how it came about that Rossiter could always penetrate the armour of her fashionable indifference and reduce her to the state of a furious and inelegant schoolgirl. "But I shan't—not before I've said one thing to you! If you *dare* to think I am such a despicable creature as to amuse myself with making a man like Captain Harries fall in love with me, I—I'll—"

Rossiter flung up a hand. "Very well!" he said ironically. "There's no need to tell me you'd blow a hole through me for my impertinence if you had the chance; we'll take that as understood. And I hope I may take it as understood, too, that you're up to no games with Miles. He's too good a man to have his heart broken by—"

"*By*—?" said Cressida, interrupting him with a dangerous light in her eyes.

"By the reigning toast of the London *ton*, who has no intention whatever of marrying him," Rossiter finished it blandly.

"And how do *you* know, pray, whom I intend to marry?" Cressida retorted crushingly, and marched away from him down the overgrown path.

But she did not go inside at once when she reached

the house. Oddly, she found herself very close to tears, and not tears of rage, but of some hopeless, lost nostalgia, engendered by the soft, still May darkness, by Rossiter's voice and presence, and by the remembrance of another spring night seven years before when she had walked with him along the prim, neat paths of her great-aunt Estella's garden in Cheltenham. How deep in love she had fancied herself then!—and now there was nothing left but bitterness, recriminations, this horrid, jarring enmity that they fell into whenever they were together!

Not that it mattered, of course—not in the least! Rossiter would marry that sly, demure little Kitty Chenevix, whom he quite deserved, and she—she would marry Langmere, and become the Queen of London Society, and live happily ever after. Obviously it was the sensible thing to do, and, with the vexed remembrance that she had left her reticule inside and her handkerchief in it, she dashed away with her hand the few hot drops which, despite this happy resolve, had persisted in welling up in her eyes and walked determinedly inside.

CHAPTER 10

"I know you will be relieved to hear, my dear," Lady Letitia confided to Cressida over the breakfast table the next morning, "that Captain Rossiter has left the house. I met Arthur as I was coming down the stairs, and he said that he—that is, Captain Rossiter—had had his curricle brought round very early this morning and has gone back to London. Why I do not know, but I cannot but think it is for the best. Perhaps, away from *his* influence, poor Arthur may be made to see the light."

Cressida, who had passed a most disagreeably wakeful night, in which she had alternated between wishing fervently that she might never set eyes upon Rossiter again and impatience for the morning to come, so that she might say all the brilliantly crushing things to him that she had unfortunately not thought of during their conversation in the garden, found herself for some reason experiencing a very strange sensation, almost one of disappointment, she might have thought, if that were not so palpably absurd, upon hearing this piece of news.

Of course she was glad that he was gone! she told herself. And to prove it, she poured herself a cup of chocolate, took a piece of buttered toast, and began to eat her breakfast as if she were feeling quite as cheerful as the birds singing outside the window in the bright May morning.

"Well, I daresay it *is* a very good thing that he has gone," she said to Lady Letitia, in what she hoped was an exceedingly calm voice, "but I don't believe we can place the least reliance upon its making any difference about Uncle Arthur's selling Calverton Place. Uncle feels he is quite powerless to do anything at all now, since the papers have already been signed, and I am bound to say that there is nothing to be hoped for from Captain Rossiter. *He* is quite determined to hold Uncle Arthur to his bargain."

The look of distressed disapproval deepened upon Lady Letitia's face.

"*So* disagreeable!" she sighed. "I had hoped, I admit, that perhaps *your* influence, my dear—After all, Captain Rossiter *was* very fond of you once. But I daresay gentlemen forget these things more easily than we weak females do."

Cressida, who was aware of the family tradition that Lady Letitia still cherished the memory of a certain Augustus Horsham, who had figured in the single romantic interlude of her otherwise tranquil existence and had behaved very badly towards her over a wealthy jeweller's daughter with a dowry of fifty thousand pounds, said rather shortly that in Rossiter's case there had been very little to forget.

"Oh, but there *was*, my dear!" Lady Letitia said earnestly, opening her faded blue eyes very wide. "I am never mistaken in such matters, I assure you. Of course, your great-aunt Estella did not think so; indeed, she made some very cutting remarks to me at the time, I remember, and said I was a great ninnyhammer and you were well rid of the man, and that it was a mere passing

fancy on his part. But I could not believe that, you see—
not after the way he behaved during that *most* distressing interview."

Cressida looked at her in some astonishment, her
cup poised midway to her lips.

"*What* interview?" she demanded. "Surely not between you and Rossiter, Cousin Letty? But you had
scarcely met him—"

"Yes, yes, I know!" Lady Letitia said, an agitated
flush rising in her thin cheeks. "Exactly what I said to
your great-aunt Estella at the time. 'I am scarcely acquainted with the man,' I said; but you *know* how in-
sistent she could be, my dear!" She looked apologetically
at Cressida. "Of course I should never have mentioned
the matter to you even now," she said, "if you weren't
quite settled at last and on the verge of accepting Langmere, as I am assured by the most *reliable* sources. I
have always been *so* afraid, you see, that it might not
have been the right thing to do—for your happiness, that
is, my dear. And then your not marrying—I have felt
quite dreadful about it at times, I assure you! But now
that it is all arranged between you and Lord Langmere—"

Cressida set down her cup.

"Cousin Letty," she said, "if you do not stop talking
in riddles and tell me exactly what you mean by all this, I
shall go mad! What *are* you talking of? *You* had some sort
of interview with Rossiter? When? At the time I was engaged to him?"

"Well, yes, my dear—but, as I've told you, it was
only because Aunt Estella quite insisted," Lady Letitia
said, looking at her piteously. "She said Arthur really
ought to do it, but that he was certain to make mice feet
of the business, and, besides, she did not at all wish him
to know that she intended to leave her entire fortune to
you. So she said I was to do it instead, because that fool
of a doctor—you *know* how she talked, my dear, though

I always thought Dr. Hurley a very sensible man myself—wouldn't permit her to do anything that might result in agitation—"

"But what *was* it that she wanted you to say to Rossiter?" Cressida demanded, feeling by this time that she really would go mad if Lady Letitia continued to talk in this vague and entirely unsatisfactory way. "And what had it to do with her leaving her fortune to me? *Pray*, Cousin Letty, *do* try to collect yourself and tell me the whole of this!"

Lady Letitia, obediently putting down her knife and fork, said she would do her best, though, really, she couldn't see that it made a great deal of difference now, since it had all happened so long ago and she—that is, Cressida—was going to marry Lord Langmere.

"You see, my love," she said patiently, "your great-aunt Estella was *quite* convinced that the chief reason for Captain Rossiter's having offered for you was his belief that she would leave her fortune to you—*not* that she had the least cause to think such a thing of him, as I myself pointed out to her, since no one, even in the family, had had the faintest inkling up to that time that she intended to leave you a penny. I am sure Arthur always considered that *he* would be the heir, and I believe he borrowed a great deal of money on the strength of his expectations—*so* disagreeable for his creditors, but then I expect they were not at all the sort of men one ought to feel sorry for, because one hears such dreadful stories about moneylenders—"

"Yes, yes!" said Cressida, seeing with alarm that if Lady Letitia was not headed off she would no doubt spend the next quarter hour happily enlarging on the theme of the inhumanity of moneylenders, with copious illustrations drawn from the experiences of the unfortunate derelicts who came within the range of her charitable works. "But Rossiter—?"

"Well, yes—Captain Rossiter," said Lady Letitia, reluctantly returning to her main subject. "I told Aunt Estella that it seemed *quite* unlikely to me that *he* could have believed you to have expectations, since no one else did; but she had taken the idea firmly in her head—you know what fancies invalids sometimes have—and nothing would do but that I should have an interview with Captain Rossiter and tell him of the arrangements she proposed to make."

"The—*arrangements*?" Cressida asked.

"Why, yes, my dear—the testamentary arrangements," Lady Letitia explained. "I was to tell him that you would inherit her entire fortune—except, of course, for a few minor bequests—in the event you *didn't* marry him, but that if you *did*, she would cut you off without a shilling. And she told me to name the amount it would come to," continued Lady Letitia, in an even lower tone than the one in which she had been speaking up to this time, "really an *enormous* sum, my love! I had had no idea, you see—she always lived so simply, quite without ostentation. And I could see that it placed Captain Rossiter in a really dreadful position. He had begun, you see, by being polite but very firm with me, and told me quite plainly that if you could not succeed in obtaining your relations' consent to your marrying him, he was prepared to wait until you came of age. But when he learned what a sacrifice you must make to marry him—well, really, my dear, I could see that the situation presented itself to him in an entirely new light. I assure you, I quite felt for him, for it was plain that his attachment to you was genuine, and that your great-aunt's decision had placed him in a *most* difficult position—"

Cressida made a stifled sound.

"Did you say something, my dear?" Lady Letitia enquired, peering at her across the table.

"No. I—" Cressida had an odd, dazed feeling that

time had rolled back seven years and she was young Cressy Calverton again, in a round gown, her hair tied with a ribbon, standing with one hip thrust out in an awkward, schoolgirl pose in the cluttered drawing room of Great-aunt Estella's Cheltenham villa, and listening with an expression of obstinate resentment upon her face as a younger and very grave Rossiter had put before her the facts of his financial situation.

"But I didn't understand!" she wanted to cry out. "I thought he was only trying to tell me that he didn't want to be poor all his life because he had married a girl with no fortune! Why didn't Great-aunt Estella tell *me* what the choice was for me? Oh, but I *know* why! Because she knew I would choose Dev, not the money, if she did, and she knew that if she left me in ignorance of the matter it would throw the whole burden upon *him*—that he must take the responsibility of choosing for me between himself and that gaudy, impossibly large fortune! And of course, whether he cared for me or not, she stood to win her game, for a fortune-hunter would never marry me if he knew I wouldn't have a penny if he did, and a man who was in love with me—Oh, how *could* she have placed him in such a position, to have to weigh what *he* could give me against that fortune—!"

She became aware, coming momentarily out of the whirling rush of her thoughts, that Lady Letitia was peering at her anxiously over the breakfast table.

"My love, are you sure you are feeling quite the thing this morning? You are looking very odd!" she said solicitously. "I hope it has not disturbed you, my bringing up this sad matter—"

"No, not in the least!" Cressida said, hastily collecting herself and coming back to present reality. "It is only —you see, I knew nothing of all this, Cousin Letty—I mean that you had talked to Captain Rossiter about Great-aunt Estella's intentions. What did he—what did he say when you told him—?"

"Well, my dear, he was very much taken-aback, of course, as well he might be," Lady Letitia said seriously. "Really, as I told you, I quite felt for him, for I could see that it placed him in a dreadful dilemma. As I said to Aunt Estella afterwards, I was persuaded that his attachment for you was genuine; but of course no gentleman with the slightest degree of principle would have pressed his suit under such circumstances. And he quite agreed with Aunt Estella's position that *you* should be kept in ignorance of the situation, as the matter was of far too great an importance to be left to a girl of eighteen to decide—"

"And so you all decided for me—you, Dev, Great-aunt Estella—that inheriting a fortune would make me far, far happier than being married to him!" Cressida burst out, suddenly unable to contain all the bitterness inside her any longer. "The three of you—Oh, I could *kill* you all!"

She got up from the table so impetuously that it tottered and the saltcellar fell over. Lady Letitia stared at her in piteous alarm.

"But, my love—dearest Cressy—you *are* happy! You are going to marry Lord Langmere!" she bleated. "It *can't* make a difference to you *now*—!"

"Well, it does!" Cressida said fiercely. "It was *my* life you were deciding, all of you—Great-aunt Estella playing God with her fortune, Dev being noble—*Dev!* I'm sure it was the only time in his life—"

Much to Lady Letitia's discomposure, she gave the table another push, as if she would have liked to up-end it entirely and send plates and cups flying, and walked out of the room.

"Oh, dear! Oh, dear!" whispered Lady Letitia, and began to cry.

As for Cressida, she seized a broad-brimmed hat, tied the ribbons beneath her chin with angry energy, and went out to walk off the agitation into which Lady

Letitia's revelations had flung her.

It was a fine May morning, bright with sunshine and gay with a bird-song, but she might have been walking through a tunnel in which she could not see her hand before her face for all the impression the surrounding landscape made upon her. It was as if her whole life, and particularly that part of it in which Rossiter had played a role, had suddenly turned topsy-turvy, so that she saw it all from a startling new perspective. Rossiter *had* cared for her then; the confrontation he had provoked with her had indeed, as she had always suspected, had the purpose of leading her to break off their engagement, but for a motive quite different from the one she had been attributing to him all these years. He had been thinking of her, not of himself, acting from chivalry—"for the first and only time in his life!" she thought vengefully. "If only he had *told* me, allowed *me* to decide—!"

But of course he had known very well, she was forced to acknowledge, what her decision would have been if he had done so. She was eighteen, and head-over-ears in love; a fortune, no matter how awe-inspiringly splendid a one, would have meant nothing to her then. But afterwards—? she could imagine Rossiter thinking. Afterwards, when she had had a taste of genteel poverty as the wife of a marching soldier, when she was older, wiser, and realised what she had thrown away—? Of course, not being a coxcomb, he would have had doubts that the happiness he was able to bring her would appear sufficient compensation to her then for what she had so hastily given up.

And so, she thought bitterly, he had stepped out of her life, leaving her with her legacy of disillusionment and the opportunity to become the immensely rich Miss Calverton, who would certainly be sought after by the most eligible *partis* in the realm. And for himself—?

She suddenly stopped dead in the middle of the

lane down which she had been unseeingly walking. There were no trees overhead here, and she became aware abruptly of a dazzle of yellow morning sunlight almost blinding her as she stood facing the east and the ascending sun. But no blinder now, she thought, than she had been these past several weeks. *Why* had he come back to England, *why* had he so persistently appeared to seek her out, *why* had he first begun calling in Mount Street? "I believe I recall hearing that you were engaged to a viscount when I visited England briefly several years ago," he had said on the occasion of their first meeting in Octavius Mayr's office. He had come back then—in the hope of a reconciliation? It might have been. And, finding her engaged to another man, he had gone off again.

And now she, still angry and bitter even after seven years, had done her best to drive him away from her again from the moment they had first come together so unexpectedly on that morning in Octavius Mayr's office. She had been brittle and cool and condescending, had refused so much as to dance with him, had turned every overture he had made to her into a challenge to battle—

"And as a result," she told herself in a cold fury, as she began to walk on slowly again towards that blinding sun-dazzle, "you have all but flung him into Kitty Chenevix's arms! What a *fool* you have been, Cressy Calverton! What a self-willed, destructive little fool! And now you will have to live with what you have done for the rest of your life!"

But even as the words said themselves in her head, she knew that they were not true. She had been a fool— yes, there was no denying that. But if anything she could do or say now had the power of erasing the effects of her stupid and odious behaviour, she was certainly going to do and say it. She had not stopped loving Dev Rossiter— it was no good not admitting that to herself now—and if there was even the remotest chance that, in spite of all her

disagreeableness to him and the disagreeableness to her
that it had evoked in return, he still cared for her as well,
she was most assuredly going to give him every opportunity to discover that his feelings were reciprocated.

The first step along this line obviously was an immediate departure from Calverton Place, and she accordingly turned her steps back at once towards the house. As
she was entering the front door she came upon Arthur
Calverton, and requested him without ceremony to send
round to the stables and have her chaise made ready at
once to leave for London.

"What—leaving already?" Mr. Calverton enquired,
looking astonished but also somewhat relieved. "I don't
know what's got into people this morning—first Rossiter
haring off at the crack of dawn, after he'd told me he was
going to stop till the end of the week, and now you—"

Cressida, coming out of her preoccupation with her
own disturbed thoughts, gave him her sudden mischievous smile.

"And *don't* tell me you won't be happy to see my
back," she said, "because I know differently. Where is
Cousin Letty? I must see her, too, before I go."

"You aren't thinking of taking her with you?" Arthur
Calverton said hopefully. "No reason for her to stop on
here now—"

"What, and wait hours for her to decide whether
she wishes to go or not and then for her to pack up her
things? I am in the greatest haste to leave, Uncle Arthur!
Please understand that, and have that message sent
round to the stables at once!"

She then walked up the stairs in search of Moodle,
leaving Mr. Calverton quite bewildered by this sudden
burning desire of hers to quit the premises, and had the
good fortune to come upon Lady Letitia just emerging
from her bedchamber with a very damp handkerchief in
her hand, into which she had been crying without inter-

ruption ever since Cressida had left the house.

"Oh, Cousin Letty, how *glad* I am to see you!" Cressida said, swooping down upon her and enveloping her in such a violently affectionate embrace that Lady Letitia was quite terrified. "I am off for London at once, but first I must thank you for telling me everything! And if things do not turn out exactly as I wish, you really must not blame yourself, for it was not in the least your fault, I know, because Great-aunt Estella could always bullock people into doing anything she wished them to!"

She then vanished into her own bedchamber, where she was immediately to be heard instructing Moodle to pack up her portmanteaux in the greatest haste. Lady Letitia, left alone and bewildered in the passage, had the dreadful feeling that somehow she had managed, by her revelations, to open Pandora's box (though what was in that mysterious casket she had not the faintest idea) and thought she might be going to cry again, but on the whole found the situation too interesting to take the time for it, and went off instead into a state of rather agitating but highly gratifying romantic speculation.

CHAPTER 11

It was not until her travelling-chaise was bowling well on its way over the grey-green Cotswold hills that it occurred to Cressida that it was all very well for her to be pelting back to London as fast as she could go, but that once she arrived there she had not the least idea how to go about attaining the object that had sent her speeding from Calverton Place in such haste.

If it had been a question of getting up an ordinary flirtation with a man—any man—she had not been six years on the town for nothing, and could have brought the matter about during a single waltz, without missing a step or causing her heart to beat a fraction of a second faster. But it was quite another thing to be obliged to inform one particular man that you had been thinking ill of him without cause for seven years, and had behaved, as a result, quite horridly to him, but that if he wished to fall in love with you now all over again, you would have not the least objection to it.

"The worst of it is," she thought despairingly, "that if I simply try to tell him quite frankly how I feel, he will undoubtedly think I am being horrid again, only in a dif-

[125]

ferent way, and that I have it in mind to do something very clever and disagreeable as soon as I have brought him round my thumb. And if he says as much to me, *I* shall certainly lose my temper and it will all end in another quarrel. Deuce take it, *why* must men be so difficult?"

Which was hardly fair to Captain Rossiter, perhaps, as he had certainly been no more difficult than had she; but then her brain was in such a whirl of astonishment, joy, and apprehension at the moment that it was not surprising that her mental processes were, on the whole, more than a little erratic.

The turmoil in her mind was not improved by the additional consideration that the first thing she must do upon reaching London was to send for Lord Langmere and inform him that under no circumstances did she now wish to avail herself of his flattering offer to make her his wife. It was an interview that she looked forward to with no pleasure at all and a considerable sense of guilt, as there could be not the least doubt that she had given his lordship a good deal of reason to expect that his suit would be successful.

However, as it was obvious that she could never convince Rossiter that she was now prepared to accept an offer from *him* unless she had previously made it crystal clear that she had no intention of accepting one from Langmere, it was a deed that had to be done, and her first care, upon reaching London just before noon on the following day, was therefore to sit down at her writing-desk and dash off a note to his lordship, requesting him to call upon her in Mount Street at his earliest convenience.

This was not accomplished without a number of interruptions from Lady Constance, who could not understand why she had had to travel all the way to Gloucestershire only to turn around and come back almost as soon as she had arrived there. She first asked a great many questions, and then told her that Rossiter had stood up for three dances with Kitty at the Russian embassy ball the night before, having arrived very late and made Drew Addison look nohow by taking her down to supper just as Addison, in his infuriatingly superior way, had signified his intention to a select circle of intimates to do her the honour of taking her down himself.

"I *do* think he—I mean Captain Rossiter, of course —is quite upon the verge of making her an offer," Lady Constance confided, with justifiable pride at the prospect of bringing such a prize catch into her protégée's net. "He has been so *very* particular in his attentions, my dear, and everyone is saying now that his buying Calverton Place proves he has the intention of settling himself permanently in England, and that dear Kitty *must* be the bride he has in mind. If only Addison does not contrive somehow to throw a rub in the way—for you know he can be a perfect *fiend* when his vanity is wounded, and he has no regard whatever for what is *comme il faut* when he is in a rage—I am quite persuaded that we shall see Kitty settled at Calverton Place before the year is out."

All this, of course, did nothing to soothe the tumult in Cressida's mind, and it was all she could do not to sit down at once and write another note, this one to Rossiter, requesting him to call in Mount Street too, so that she could tell him how her feelings towards him had changed.

But this was manifestly quite impossible; *that* was a matter that would require far more subtlety than the frank statement she must make to Lord Langmere. She was pleased to gather from Lady Constance's conversation, at any rate, that she was certain to see Rossiter if she attended the ball to be given that evening by Lady Maybridge in honour of one of the visiting German princelings, as he had signified his intention to be present at it; and she accordingly determined to possess her soul in patience until that time.

Meanwhile, there was Lord Langmere to be faced, who presented himself in Mount Street, with loverlike impatience, a mere half hour after her message to him had been delivered.

"No—don't!" she was obliged to say to him hastily, putting out both hands to ward off the embrace in which he attempted to enfold her as she trod into the drawing room, where Harbage had bestowed him. "Leonard—dear Leonard, you are at liberty to think me the greatest wretch alive, but I must tell you at once—I cannot marry you. I have had time to think it all over very carefully now, and *indeed* it will not do!"

To say that Lord Langmere was taken aback by this forthright and determined statement would give but a very inadequate impression of his feelings at that moment. There was no room here for hoping that what he had just heard was the blushful temporising of a young lady who was waiting only to be urged to change her mind; he was obliged to believe that he was being given his *congé*, and that Cressida had no intention whatever of altering her resolution in the matter.

Lord Langmere was a mild-mannered man, and to have said that he was deeply in love would have been dignifying by too strong a term, perhaps, his admiration of the dashing Miss Calverton, his pride in having been able to exhibit her preference for him before the world, and his quite genuine intention to settle himself in life with her and to make her the most exemplary of husbands. But even mild-mannered men who are mildly in love do not take kindly to having all their expectations overturned in the twinkling of an eye, and it was therefore scarcely surprising that, as a consequence, a rather painful scene took place in the drawing room of the

Mount Street house. His lordship so far forgot himself as to insinuate with some bitterness that he had been led down the garden path; Cressida, though conscious that he spoke with some justice, was much too full of her own troubles to sympathise properly with his, and as a result neglected to sooth him down with asseverations of her undying regard and other bits of flattering nonsense that would at least have sent him away with the comforting conviction that he had been engaging in a star-crossed romance instead of merely making a fool of himself over a heartless flirt.

Accordingly, a quarter hour after he had entered the drawing room he left it hastily and in an obviously black mood, almost caroming into Kitty in the hall, who regarded him thoughtfully and then went on into the drawing room herself to tell Cressida, whom she had not seen since the latter's return, how pleased she was to have her so soon back in London.

Cressida, who felt that, of all the people in the world she did not wish to see at that moment, Kitty stood highest on the list, said shortly that she was glad to be back, and then added more kindly, wrenching her thoughts with some effort from the scene with Lord Langmere, that she hoped Kitty had been enjoying herself while she had been gone.

"Oh yes, Miss Calverton!" said Kitty, in such a quiet, natural voice that Cressida, who had just had a sudden, rather unpleasant sensation that Kitty's blue eyes had been regarding her with a sharp and somewhat speculative intensity, thought she must have been mistaken. "I can never thank you enough for giving me such a splendid opportunity," Kitty continued, her eyes, now radiating sincerity, raised earnestly to Cressida's.

Cressida wondered momentarily what change might occur in that modest, self-assured demeanour if she were to inform its possessor of the conversation that had taken place between her and Mrs. Mills in Keppel Street, but, being conscious of a certain duplicity in her own behaviour in not informing Kitty frankly of the fact that she intended to do everything in her power to take Rossiter away from her, she scarcely felt that it behooved her to animadvert upon anyone else's conduct at the moment, and went upstairs to her bedchamber in a rather low mood. This was not improved by the fact that it had just begun to rain in a depressingly steady way that made it quite obvious that it was determined to continue to do so for at least four-and-twenty hours.

Nor were her spirits raised, as the hour approached at which she was to leave for the Maybridges' ball, and therefore to meet Rossiter for the first time since her feelings towards him had so markedly changed, by the onslaught of a sensation of nervous self-consciousness such as she believed herself to have outgrown years before. She could not decide on which gown to wear, rejected an orange-blossom sarsnet as too missish and a water-green silk as too daring, had Moodle dress her hair in a Sappho and then *à la Tite*, and as a result kept the Honourable Drew Addison, who had condescended to gallant the Mount Street ladies to the ball, cooling his heels in the drawing room with Kitty and Lady Constance for almost half an hour. This brought down upon her several waspish comments, to which she replied so absently that Addison, who was unaccustomed to seeing his barbs fly wide of their target, was irritated all over again.

"I gather, my dear Cressy, that you had no success in persuading the not-so-gallant Captain to give up Calverton Place to you," he observed pointedly, as he seated himself beside her in the carriage. "No, don't look surprised, my good child; of course I know all about the reason for that sudden excursion of yours into Gloucestershire. I also know," he continued suavely as the carriage rolled off down the street, "that Langmere has at last put his fate to the touch and been given his *congé*. Oh yes, my dear; he was at White's this afternoon, and in such a fit of the blue-devils that one could not help putting two and two together. I believe he won two thousand from Dalingridge at hazard. *Unlucky in love,* you know—"

Here Lady Constance, who could no longer contain herself upon hearing this startling and most unwelcome piece of news (for Cressida had said nothing to her of what had passed between her and Lord Langmere that day), burst into the conversation to demand what in the world Addison meant by making such an absurd and totally untrue statement.

"Of course nothing of the sort has occurred," she scolded him, "and I beg you will not go about repeating such a faradiddle to everyone you meet! It is true that there is no understanding *as yet* between Cressida and Langmere—"

"Nor ever will be," Addison said languidly. "Am I not right, Cressy, my dearest? You have laid another of your victims in the dust, and now have certainly no wish—having shown yourself the goddess triumphant once more—to raise him."

"*Do* stop talking such fustian, Drew!" Cressida said coldly. "One would think you had been indulging in reading lending library novels—which you profess to abhor!"

"And so I do, my sweet," said Addison, smiling at her calmly. "But if one's friends *will* persist in behaving as if they belonged between the covers of those revoltingly sentimental works, what is one to do? You really *must* break yourself of the habit of leading besotted males to the very brink of matrimony and then baulking at the last moment at stepping over the edge with them, Cressy darling; it always leads to low drama in the general conversation."

Cressida, who had hoped to be able to explain to

Rossiter herself in a very dignified manner that she and
Langmere had mutually agreed that they would not suit,
and that any thought of marriage between them was now
at an end, felt her heart sink. From Addison's words it
was perfectly apparent that her rejection of Lord Langmere's suit would be one of the principal topics of conversation at the ball that evening, so that Rossiter would
be certain to be treated upon every side with the most
highly coloured interpretation of her conduct that gossip,
and sometimes malicious gossip, could give it. A heartless jilt—that was what would be said of her; and Rossiter himself had as much as pronounced those very words
in the garden at Calverton Place. How was she to explain
to him, in a crowded ballroom, that it was only because
she had rediscovered her love for him that she had given
Langmere his dismissal? If only she might see him
alone—

But the impossibility of achieving such a wish on
this evening, of all others, was made abundantly clear to
her as the carriage entered Cavendish Square, which
was the scene at the moment of an even greater
confusion than ordinarily attended the hour of arrival at a
large ball. Lady Maybridge's parties were famous for
being the greatest squeezes of the Season, and the
Square was already filled with a crush of jostling carriages and excited horses when they arrived, so that it
seemed next to impossible that they would ever be able
even to reach the door of Maybridge House.

"Tiresome!" commented Addison, regarding with
some distaste the efforts of a swearing coachman driving
an elegant town-chariot with a crest upon the panel to
force his way in before them in the line of carriages that
was slowly crawling along the street. "One does so
wonder if it is worth the effort to make an appearance at
one of Gussie Maybridge's balls. Even when one suc-
ceeds in getting inside, one is always at least half an hour

on the staircase, pressed in cheek by jowl, as like as not, with some quite unconversable foreign ambassador, with his wife's ostrich plumes tickling one's nose. Unfortunately, one cannot consider attending a party that is so very unsuccessful that one can enter the house with ease. It would be too drearily unfashionable—"

He went on speaking, but Cressida was no longer attending to him. She had caught sight, through the slanting, silvery rain, of a tall figure just alighting from a carriage that had that moment drawn up before the doorway of Maybridge House. She could see only the broad shoulders, the erect back, and the well-shaped head with its severely cropped black hair, but she knew she could not be mistaken. It was Rossiter, and if only, she thought, in sudden wild, hopeful impatience, Addison's coachman would make haste to bring their carriage up to the door, she might manage to spend that interminable half hour upon the crowded staircase, to which Addison had alluded, in such close proximity to him that something of what she wished to inform him about her change in feelings might be conveyed to him, in spite of foreign ambassadors, their wives, *and* their wives' ostrich plumes.

CHAPTER 12

Of course nothing so fortunate occurred. Instead, she was obliged, during the five-and-twenty minutes she spent ascending, step by step, the magnificent red-carpeted staircase of Maybridge House, to endure the torments of Tantalus, seeing Rossiter's dark head directly before her the whole time, but separated from her by the stout and exceedingly solid bulk of a lady in a puce satin gown and a diamond tiara. By the time she had reached the head of the staircase he had already exchanged greetings with Lord and Lady Maybridge and passed on into the ballroom, and seeking for him there, she knew, amidst upwards of six hundred people, half of whom were dancing, while the other half milled about in a kaleidoscopic fashion behind the red-velvet ropes that divided the dance-floor from the rest of the room, would certainly be a tedious and perhaps unsuccessful task.

To her discomfort, the first person she *did* see was Lord Langmere, who was pressed, willy-nilly, almost directly up to her in the crush, bowed slightly to her with a somewhat heightened colour, and immediately made the most determined effort to escape from her presence.

"So you haven't given him his marching orders!" Addison's cynical voice said behind her. "Dearest Cressy, do you think me *quite* muttonheaded, that you expect me to swallow such a rapper as that? He had as well be wearing a placard reading *Rejected Lover* on the back of his coat! And what odds," he added thoughtfully, "will you give me that young Harries won't be the next to succeed to his honours? The bettors at White's, I may tell you, will be badly scorched if he is not: he has been so much in your company of late that a good many of them are plunging heavily on him. But here he comes now. Will you stand up to dance with him and swing the odds even more in his favour, or do you intend to cause a panic by snubbing him?"

Cressida felt that if it were possible and legal to kill someone in a ballroom, the odds were that Drew Addison would be dead at that moment by her hand, but she was obliged to content herself with ignoring him as completely as if she had not heard a word he had spoken, and greeted Captain Harries with great cordiality instead.

"Good evening, Miss Calverton; I'd like very much to ask you to do me the honour of standing up with me for the next dance," said the Captain, who looked, as usual, rather harassed by the responsibility of living up to his elegant coat and knee breeches but very pleased to see her. "But they tell me it's to be the quadrille, and for the life of me I haven't been able to master the steps."

He then looked at Kitty, who appeared to the greatest advantage that evening in a robe of pale blue crape caught together down the front with small silver clasps over a white sarsnet slip, and he was obviously about to address himself to her when, Addison having dropped a few words into her ear, she turned to Lady Constance and very prettily asked her permission to stand up for the quadrille with him. Lady Constance looked disapproving, but she was too well aware of the power Addison wielded in Society to cross swords with him, and, with a slight, expressive shrug of her shoulders, gave her consent.

"Detestable man!" she said, as the two walked off together. "He is only singling her out for his attentions to set Rossiter on end, and though I am as well aware as the next person that there is nothing like a little jealousy to bring *some* gentlemen to the point, Rossiter does *not* appear to me to be that sort of man. If Kitty is not careful, she will find she has whistled him down the wind."

She broke off to greet a dowager in purple-bloom silk, with whom she at once moved away down the room. Cressida looked at Captain Harries.

"I see," she said, "that you have not been having a great deal of success while I have been away."

The Captain, looking downcast, said no, he had not.

"But I'm bound to say," he added, plucking up his spirits slightly, "that, with Dev away, too, it's that Addison fellow who's been claiming most of her time, and they say there's safety in numbers."

"Perhaps there is," said Cressida, suddenly feeling an irresistible urge to confide her difficulties to the Captain, who was, after all, in much the same dilemma as she was herself, and had as much interest as she had in seeing to it that Rossiter did not marry Kitty. "But it's a great deal like playing hazard: there is always the chance that the very number one particularly does not wish to will turn up!"

She glanced about impatiently at the long, crowded room: it was quite useless, she saw, to expect that anywhere within its brilliant confines she might have a few minutes of private, uninterrupted conversation with her companion. But she was familiar with Maybridge House, and remembered suddenly that, behind the heavy crimson brocade draperies before which they were at present standing, there was a shallow embrasure leading to one of the ballroom's long double windows, each of which had built outside it a narrow balcony enclosed by a low iron railing.

"I should like to talk to you—come along!" she said to the Captain, parting the heavy draperies and passing swiftly into the embrasure.

The Captain obediently followed her, unbolted and flung open the long window at her direction, and then stepped outside with her onto the narrow covered ledge beyond.

"This is far better!" Cressida said, much relieved, and looking about her at the misty darkness. She felt, in fact, so very much relieved, after Addison's disagreeable words and the knowledge that at that precise moment some equally nasty-minded person was undoubtedly pouring into Rossiter's ears the most unpleasant version he or she could concoct of her dismissal of Langmere, that she experienced a sudden desire to put her head upon the Captain's broad, comforting shoulder and wail out her troubles like a schoolgirl. "Oh!" she said, bringing herself up short before she could give way to this ignoble impulse, "you will think I am an idiot, Captain Harries, but I simply *must* tell someone. I have just learned, you see, that while I was thinking all these years that Dev wished to break off our engagement because of not wanting to marry a girl with no money, he really did it only because he had been told that I shouldn't inherit my great-aunt's fortune if I married him. And it has made me feel quite, quite different about him, of course, and—and I don't at all wish him to marry Kitty Chenevix now, any more than you wish him to do so. Only everyone says he is quite on the point of offering for her, and—oh, Captain Harries, what *are* we to do?"

Captain Harries, who had hitherto been in the way of regarding Miss Calverton as the sort of goddesslike female who was so capable of managing her own affairs to her entire satisfaction that any male interference in them would be not only unnecessary but impertinent, was shocked beyond measure to find a face that distinctly appeared to be upon the verge of tears turned up in despairing appeal to his. But he recovered himself quickly, and, much touched, put his arm around Cressida in an extremely comforting and brotherly way and said he had suspected it all along.

"Suspected what?" said Cressida in a rather muffled voice, giving herself up in an unwonted way to the luxury of having someone to lean on in her distress.

"That you were in love with him, and he with you," said the Captain simply.

"Oh!" Cressida exclaimed, looking up at him with a radiant face. "Oh, do you *really* think so?"

And at that precise moment the draperies parted suddenly and Rossiter walked into the embrasure.

The tableau he saw before him at that instant—the dashing Miss Calverton, her waist encircled by a manly arm, gazing up radiantly into the face of her companion —was one he could have been pardoned for misconstruing; in point of fact, it was scarcely possible that he could have avoided misinterpreting it. He remained standing for a moment, thunderstruck, his arm still raised to hold back the draperies, so that the brilliant candlelight from the ballroom streamed full upon the startled pair before him. Then he said, in a harsh, even voice, "I beg your pardon! I came to ask you to dance, Miss Calverton. I was not aware that you were otherwise engaged."

"But I wasn't—I mean I'm not—" Cressida, finding her tongue, stammered, quite idiotically, as she was furiously aware.

Rossiter's contemptuous gaze scorched her. "Good God," he exclaimed savagely, "don't think to shuffle Miles aside now while you attempt to add *me* to your list of conquests for the evening! Isn't it enough that you have made Langmere a laughingstock, without wishing to do the same for him?"

And without another word he stepped back into the ballroom and let the draperies fall to behind him. The light was cut off abruptly; in the damp, late spring darkness Cressida and Captain Harries faced each other, pale and aghast.

"I'd best go after him and explain—" the Captain began hastily, at the same moment that Cressida said in a stifled voice, "I *must* explain—"

Then they both stopped speaking, a look of dismayed realisation appearing simultaneously upon both their faces.

"We can't possibly!" Cressida said despairingly. "He will never believe that I brought you out here only to tell you I am in love with *him*! He will think we are merely making game of him!"

The Captain, to whom the same idea appeared to have occurred, looked shaken, but said he had best have a try at it, all the same.

"No, don't!" said Cressida anxiously. "Not just now, at any rate. He is in a black rage—can't you see? He won't listen to you, and if you try to defend me, he will think it is because I have b-bewitched you— Deuce take it, I am *not* going to cry!" she said, searching angrily in her reticule for a handkerchief. "That ghastly Addison will be certain to notice if I do, and say I am regretting having turned Langmere off, or something beastly like that."

To Captain Harries's considerable respect, she blew her nose defiantly, said she was all right now, and they had better go back to the ballroom.

"I'd go straight home, but I can't, because of Kitty and Lady Con, and besides, people would be sure to talk," she said. "We *must* go back, and pretend that everything is perfectly normal, and then perhaps tomorrow, when he is not so *very* angry any longer, you can contrive to talk to him—"

The Captain, who was looking more dubious by the moment as the full force of the difficulties of such an interview struck him, said he would do his best, but what was he to say to him?

"I don't *know*," said Cressida, hitting her eyes angrily with her handkerchief. "I suppose it might help a bit if you were to tell him you weren't at all in love with me, but with Kitty—"

The Captain looked horrified. "But I couldn't do that!" he said earnestly. "Not when he—he may be attached to her himself!"

And then, aware that he had said quite the wrong thing, he coloured up furiously; but Cressida, who was by this time in full command of herself again, only said decisively that he wasn't, and if he was, he oughtn't to be.

"If he were so idiotish as to marry her, he would probably murder her before the honeymoon was over," she said. "He hasn't an angelic temper, like you, and he can't endure people who bore him, or lie to him. She would be certain to do both. When I was still angry with him, I was used to think it would serve him right if he *did* marry her, as then he would be just as fiendishly unhappy as *I* was when he made me break off our engagement. But I don't want him to be unhappy now."

Captain Harries both looked and felt extremely shocked by all this plain speaking, especially the part that reflected upon his inamorata, but as he had the kind of frank, simple character that is able to face imperfection in the beloved object without being shaken in the least in its stubborn adoration, he forgave Miss Calverton quickly, as not being quite herself at the moment, and said comfortingly that he was sure matters would all come right in the end.

"Perhaps they will, but just as likely they won't,"

said Cressida, who was far more inclined to take a realistic view of the situation.

But this did not in the least mean that she had resigned herself to failure, for she was already revolving plans in her mind for seeing to it that matters *did* come right, if they were at all amenable to being pushed into their proper place by her.

As no good purpose could be served, however, by her remaining any longer now upon the narrow balcony with Captain Harries, she sent him back into the ballroom with the strict injunction to ask Kitty to stand up with him for the next dance and as many more as he could secure from her, and followed him herself after a short, discreet interval.

Rossiter was nowhere to be seen when she emerged from behind the crimson brocade draperies and surveyed the thronged ballroom, nor could she catch a glimpse of either Kitty or Lady Constance, so she allowed herself to be led into a set of country dances by her latest admirer, a young and very dashing captain in the Dragoon Guards. He had obviously heard the news of her dismissal of Lord Langmere, and was so much emboldened by it that he became quite embarrassingly ardent even under the severe restrictions imposed upon him by the movement of the dance, and at the conclusion of the set at once importuned her to allow him the privilege of taking her down to supper later in the evening.

But his right to this honour was immediately disputed by half a dozen other gentlemen who had been awaiting the end of the dance to approach her, and she was standing smiling and debating among all these offers when a new claimant, a young baronet, joined the group.

"I say," he remarked in a bored drawl that belied the flush of interested excitement upon his face, "the most extraordinary thing! Rossiter has proposed to Miss Chenevix and been accepted. Never ask me where he found the opportunity in this squeeze—but I daresay he's not the sort to let a little matter like privacy stand in his way—"

The smile froze upon Cressida's lips, and the sounds, sights, and perfumes of the brilliant, crowded room seemed to rush all together to form a single sensation of exploding light and colour, which, combined with what appeared to be a highly unusual rocking motion of the floor beneath her feet, made her feel for a moment as if she were on a boat in a storm on tropical seas. When she recovered herself enough to speak, the questions she would have liked to put to the young baronet had already been asked by others, and the young man was replying to the best of his ability.

"I had it from Lady Con Havener, so it must be true," he said. "She is in the card-room, telling everyone who will listen to her. Addison is looking as blue as megrim. Of course everyone knows he has been casting out lures to the girl himself—"

He halted abruptly as Cressida, saying, "In the card-room?" in a rather dazed voice, walked right through him, like a sleepwalker, or at least looked as if she would have done if he had not moved aside in nimble astonishment. She made her way towards the end of the ballroom, where a pair of doors led to a saloon that had been set out with tables for the convenience of those guests who cared more for cards than for dancing. Like the ballroom, it was crowded to the walls with players and onlookers, and was even more insufferably hot. Cressida found Lady Constance seated upon a sofa at the end of the room, with half a dozen ladies and gentlemen gathered about her, and went straight up to her.

"Lady Con," she said, "I must talk to you."

"Yes, dear," said Lady Constance, obligingly moving to try to make a place for her upon the sofa beside her, and looking as proud as a mother cat who has produced a splendid litter of kittens. "Oh, Cressy, my love, *have* you heard what has happened? Rossiter has—"

"Not here," said Cressida firmly, and to the surprise and admiration of all beholders, who knew that nothing was more difficult than to move Lady Constance when she was settled for a comfortable gossip, particularly when she herself was cast in the role of the star of the piece, she got her to her feet by the sheer power of command of the gaze she bent upon her, out of the card-room, across the ballroom floor, and out onto one of the same narrow balconies on which her unfortunate interview with Captain Harries had taken place.

"But isn't it dangerous?" Lady Constance, who was nervous of even moderate heights, enquired as she glanced apprehensively over the narrow iron railing.

"No," said Cressida. "But *I* shall be if you don't tell me at once exactly what has happened. Has Rossiter—?"

"Well, my dear, I was *trying* to tell you in the card-room, when you made me come out here instead," Lady Constance said in an aggrieved voice. "But yes—he *has* actually made Kitty an offer—while they were engaged in a set of country dances, if you will credit it! *Most* extraordinary—but then he *is* an extraordinary man, I believe! Everyone heard him—I mean all the people who were next them in the set—and I *do* think it reflects well upon Kitty's good sense that she was not totally overset—"

"She accepted him?" Cressida interrupted, in an abrupt, rather stifled voice.

"Well, my dear, not precisely there in the set, of course!" Lady Constance said virtuously. "She brought him to me after it was over, and asked me very prettily what she was to do—though it was quite apparent, of course, what she *wished* to do. And I naturally said that they must consult her mama, who is her proper guardian, but that, standing as I did in her place at present, *I* could see no possible objection, and was quite sure

Emily Chenevix would feel as I did, that it was a *most* suitable match—"

"And so you have been spreading the story of an engagement to everyone in this ballroom—which means all of London!" Cressida interrupted her again, in a shaking voice. "Oh, Lady Con, you *are* a widgeon!"

"Well, I am sure I do not know why you should say *that!*" said Lady Constance, looking affronted. "I think I have been very clever! You may say what you like, my love, but it is always best to pin a man down in these cases, for no matter how ardent they may be, they *will* sometimes have second thoughts. And, besides, it isn't as if he wasn't *overheard* making her the offer—Why, my dear, what *is* the matter?" she broke off to ask, suddenly becoming aware, even in the darkness, of the tragedy on Cressida's face and the tears glittering in her eyes. She looked at her with dawning comprehension and dismay. "You can't mean that *you*—that *he*—"

"Yes—no! It doesn't signify!" said Cressida, very disjointedly and in a muffled voice, turning her head away to hide her face from observation.

Lady Constance, who was truly quite thunderstruck by this development, for the idea had literally never entered her head that the old attachment between Cressida and Rossiter was not entirely a thing of the past, continued to stare at her in the greatest puzzlement.

"But, my dear, I don't in the least understand!" she protested at length. "You have never shown the least partiality for Captain Rossiter; indeed, it has always seemed to me that the two of you come to dagger-drawing every time you meet! And if *he* cares for *you*, why did he offer to Kitty—?"

"Oh, I can't explain! It is all such a *confounded* muddle!" Cressida said angrily. "*I* don't know what is to be done—nothing, I daresay, now that it has been published all over London that he has made her an offer! He couldn't cry off now, even if he wished to—and Kitty won't—We had best go back to the ballroom," she broke off abruptly. "There can be no purpose served by discussing this any further!"

"Yes, but—" Lady Constance looked at her with an expression of some doubt upon her face. "Are you quite sure—? I have asked Captain Rossiter to join us for supper, of course, and it will not appear at all proper for you to ignore the whole matter and go on as if nothing had happened, since Kitty *is* staying in your house—"

"Very well! *I* shall join you for supper, too!" Cressida said, in grim resignation. "But I warn you that we shall all be *very* uncomfortable! Rossiter is furious with me, you see!"

"He is? But I thought that you—that he—"

Lady Constance gave it up, and with a helpless shrug followed Cressida back into the ballroom. Here the latter was at once seized upon by the admirers she had disappointed by going off so hurriedly into the cardroom in search of Lady Constance, and, having awarded the waltz that was just then beginning to the young baronet who had brought the news of Rossiter's engagement, she chose the oldest of the group, a well-known diplomatist, to take her down to supper afterwards, feeling that his experience best fitted him to cope with the sort of disagreeable situation into which he would be thrust.

And disagreeable it certainly was. Rossiter, looking grim, was pointedly attentive to his chosen bride; Lady Constance, for once thrown quite off her stride, socially speaking, chattered indefatigably and pointlessly; Cressida was far too gay and did not once meet Rossiter's eyes; and the diplomatist, who, with the sixth sense of his profession, realised he was in deep waters, prudently retired into his shell like a tortoise and contributed nothing to the conversation except an occasional smile or shrug of his shoulders.

Only Kitty looked as serene as always, with a pretty, deprecatory air when she addressed her affianced husband that did not quite conceal, Cressida considered, a certain quiet triumph. She had got what she wanted: that was plain—a husband, a fortune, and an assured position in Society. It must have seemed to her, Cressida thought, that the small deception she had had to perpetrate to obtain them was an insignificant price to pay for them.

"And isn't she *quite* the princess at the end of the fairy tale," Addison, who had been going about all evening making cleverly disparaging remarks about the newly betrothed couple, said in Cressida's ear as they were leaving a little later, "with nothing to do but live happily ever after? Only one *does* so wonder about the prince—doesn't one? A rather ramshackle sort of royalty —don't you agree?—in spite of all that vulgar money. Kitty, my admired love," he broke off as Kitty appeared with Lady Constance, ready for the drive back to Mount Street, "my deepest felicitations to you. You shall ride in a carriage and wear a silk gown—which, of course, you are about to do at present, I may note, and with me, but *not*, my sweet, with a ring upon your finger. We shall have to see about that presently."

Cressida looked up at him quickly, but there was nothing to be read in that cold, selfish, handsome face but the urbane mockery usually present there. No doubt it was quite mad of her, she thought, to expect any help from that direction, for even if Addison was disgruntled by Rossiter's having carried Kitty off in spite of his own attentions to her, he would never offer marriage to her himself.

She got into the carriage drearily with Kitty and Lady Constance, and it was not until all of ten minutes had passed, and the coachman had disentangled his vehicle from the horrible crush of traffic in the Square without having it suffer the fate of a cabriolet just before them, which had somehow got the hind legs of one of its horses enmeshed in the fore-wheel of a barouche, that her natural optimism reasserted itself and she made up her mind that, after all, the battle was not lost until the fatal words had been pronounced in church. And if she had to lose it in the end, she thought, she might at least have the satisfaction of going down fighting.

CHAPTER 13

It did not take her long to realise, however, that if she was to continue the battle she must have allies who could supply both advice and assistance. Lady Constance, she considered, with her loyalties divided between sympathy for Cressida's plight and rejoicing over Kitty's triumph, was useless in this respect, and she therefore made up her mind that very night to place her reliance instead upon Sir Octavius. She had once told Lady Constance that he was the wisest man she knew, and certainly, it appeared to her, the wisdom of a Solomon would be required to untangle the extraordinary muddle into which her affairs had got themselves.

On the following morning, accordingly, she sent a message to Sir Octavius enquiring if she might consult him on a matter of the utmost importance, and, having received a prompt affirmative response, she was about to leave the house for the City when she was interrupted by the arrival of Lady Dalingridge.

"I shall just stay for the *tiniest* moment, Cressy dear!" said Lady Dalingridge, who had observed Cressida's bonnet and gloves and the carriage waiting before the door, but had no intention of allowing them to stay her in her course. "I have come, you see, only to warn you of that *charming snake,* Addison—one of the most irreistible men I have ever met, of course, my dear, but quite madly *orgueilleux,* as you know yourself. I remember Prince Pückler-Muskau saying once—you *do* recall Pückler, don't you?—one of the few really *attractive* Germans we have had over here, I have always said, and it never surprised me that he came within amesace of carrying off Lady Lansdowne and her fortune before her daughter thrust a spoke into his wheel—but, at any rate, he was used to say that he could *not* understand why our English dandies felt called upon to avenge even the most unimportant social slight in the most *vindictive* way. Really quite appalling, it appeared to him, and I must say that in Addison's case it is *not* an exaggeration. *Do* you think he might find some excuse now to call Rossiter out?"

"Not," said Cressida impatiently, "unless he wishes to make himself ridiculous by giving notice to the world that he cares whether Rossiter marries Kitty or not. And now, Dolly, I really must—"

"—go. Yes, I know," said Lady Dalingridge obligingly, but making no move to arise from the very comfortable armchair in which she had seated herself. "And I really shan't keep you more than a *moment* longer—only I thought you and Lady Con *ought* to know, since you are in the way of being responsible for Miss Chenevix at present, that they are laying bets at White's that Addison will have the girl in the end, after all. Dalingridge was there after the Maybridge ball last night, and he says the affair has caused the most extraordinry brouhaha—which is no great wonder, of course, because everyone has *seen* from the start that Addison was quite green over Rossiter's having been taken up by the *ton* without *his* approval, and then this affair of the girl—"

"Yes—well, you must tell Lady Con all about it; I can hear her coming downstairs now," said Cressida, still more impatiently; and she made good her escape and went out to her carriage.

She was shown into Sir Octavius's office at once when she arrived, and it was not until she had sat down in her favourite gondola armchair and heard his first quizzical enquiry as to what had brought her to him in such urgent haste that it occurred to her that she had no idea how to begin upon her tale, or what she expected Sir Octavius to do when she had finished it.

To her intense surprise, however, Sir Octavius, seeing her at a loss, at once began upon the matter himself.

"I hear," he remarked, with a kindly air, "that Rossiter has asked Miss Chenevix to marry him."

Cressida stared at him. "Yes, he has," she said. "But how did you—?"

"How did I know it was that affair that you had come to see me about in such alarmed haste? Really, my dear Cressy, you must not take me for a complete clothhead," Sir Octavius said, leaning back comfortably in his chair, his dark eyes amused. "It has been perfectly obvious to me from the first time I saw you and Rossiter together in this office that the two of you were top-over-tail in love with each other. Nothing else would account for the quite ferocious rudeness of your manner towards each other. And why else," he continued inexorably, as Cressida attempted to put in a word, "do you think I informed you, as soon as I heard of it, that Rossiter was buying Calverton Place, except to send you after him and give you both every opportunity to quarrel yourselves to a standstill and then make up your differences, as people in love are so frequently apt to do? I gather that in this case, though, the plot failed to achieve its purpose."

"Yes, it did," Cressida said with some asperity. "So

you needn't have been so devious, after all. I loathe and despise devious people!"

"Which is exactly why you have come to me today," Sir Octavius said mildly. "But very well, then—since you so much prefer frankness, why don't you simply tell Rossiter that you are in love with him and would like him to marry you instead of Miss Chenevix?"

"As if I could—or *would*—do such a thing!" Cressida said indignantly. "You know that is utterly impossible!"

"Do I?" said Sir Octavius. He shrugged his shoulders. "Well, perhaps I do. We should have no three-volume novels if characters came straight to the point and said exactly what was on their minds, and people in real life are so tiresomely apt to behave in the same way, quite as if they had been made up by an author with more pages to fill than matter to put into them. Very well; my second piece of advice to you, then, is to find someone else for Miss Chenevix."

"But I have! I mean, there is someone!" Cressida said. "Captain Harries is very sincerely attached to her, and would marry her tomorrow if she would have him. But he is nowhere near as rich as Dev, and I am sure she will never consider marrying him as long as she can have Dev instead."

"All of which," Sir Octavius said, looking at her with his right eyebrow raised very high, "sounds as if you were remarkably certain that Miss Chenevix is not marrying for love."

"Well, she isn't," Cressida said decidedly. "In point of fact, I shouldn't think it's likely she knows what it is to fall in love, or ever will. She is one of those ambitious, comfort-loving creatures, like a cat, who will always be concerned only with seeing that she has the largest saucer of cream and the softest velvet cushion in the house. And if that makes *me* sound like the biggest cat in Christendom," she added reflectively, "I really can't help it, because it is true."

"Never having met the young lady, I am not able to give an opinion in the matter," Sir Octavius said. "But I *do* know Rossiter, and I should say it was in the highest degree unlikely that he should have captivated a young lady of the description you have given. If Miss Chenevix were romantically inclined, that, of course, would be another matter: he has all the ingredients necessary to inspire a fatal passion in a young lady of *that* turn of mind. But in a girl of a—as you have so eloquently described it —feline temperament, no. He is far too brusque-mannered to inspire anything but distaste in her. So if you are right, it is merely his fortune and position that are attracting her, and it therefore seems to me that we shall be quite justified in thrusting a spoke into her wheel."

Cressida said rather despairingly that she would like very much to thrust in several, if she thought there was the least chance Rossiter still cared for her; but she could not be at all sure of that.

"You see, he thinks I have behaved very badly about Langmere, and so I have, only I never should have done if *he* hadn't come back to England," she said. "And *now* he thinks I am in love with Miles Harries, or at least that I am trying to lure him into my clutches, like a villainess in a melodrama."

"Good God, why should he think that?" Sir Octavius enquired, and Cressida told him rather guiltily about the scene on the balcony at the Maybridges' the night before.

"I *don't* know," said Sir Octavius resignedly, when she had concluded, "why things of that sort always appear to happen to you. I daresay it is because you are so devastatingly attractive that men can't help thinking the worst of you. If you were plain, now, it would make matters a great deal simpler for me."

Cressida said rather rebelliously that if she were plain Rossiter wouldn't wish to marry her.

"Oh yes, he would," Sir Octavius said. "He fell in love with you when you were—I won't say plain, for that you never were, but a hobbledehoy schoolgirl with not the faintest notion of how to dress or carry yourself, exactly as you were when I saw you first. And now you have turned into the dashing Miss Calverton, with all London at your feet, and of course he thinks you are a heartless Jezebel." He sighed. "Very well," he said, "you may dine with me on Wednesday next—you, and Miss Chenevix, and, if you can persuade her, Lady Constance. I shall send cards to Rossiter and Harries, too, of course. It will be a very uncomfortable dinner-party, but I daresay no worse than most."

Cressida stared at him. "But why a dinner-party?" she enquired. "What purpose will that possibly serve—?"

"For one thing, my dear, it will bring you and Rossiter together in the same room without five or six hundred other people there as well to complicate matters," Sir Octavius said. "And for another, it will give you something to occupy your mind over the next several days while Rossiter and Miss Chenevix go through the process—as we must devoutly hope they will—of discovering that being engaged to each other is not quite so agreeable as they may have imagined it would be. And in the third place, it will give me an opportunity to meddle, which is why you came to me in the first place, isn't it? So go away now, my good child; I am very busy this morning, and have no more time to devote to love's complications!"

This speech sent Cressida home in a rather chastened, but much more hopeful, mood, and as she had great reliance upon Sir Octavius, she was able to face the ensuing days quite well, with their inevitable accompaniment of congratulatory calls upon Kitty, Lady Constance's vacillations between being very proud of herself and guilty interludes of feeling she had ruined Cressida's life, and Rossiter's occasional presence in the house when he came to take Kitty for a drive in the Park.

It did not escape Cressida's notice that, after these latter excursions, Kitty returned to the house looking notably subdued. She never confided to either Cressida or Lady Constance the circumstances that had caused this, but Cressida heard from Dolly Dalingridge that Rossiter had on one occasion encouraged his affianced bride to take the reins of his phaeton in an effort to teach her to drive, and that she had shown herself so inept a pupil that he had restrained his temper with difficulty, treated her to a brief, biting lecture, and promised never to allow her to handle any of his cattle again.

"And after that, of course," Dolly had continued, "Addison must come up to them on that splendid new bay of his and begin paying the girl the most extravagantly *galant* compliments, so that he drew her quite out of the combination of sulks and terrors she had fallen into. If you wish *my* opinion, she is far more *éprise* with him than she has ever been with Rossiter, and no wonder, for he lays himself out to be at his most charming whenever he is with her. And Rossiter sat there paying them not the slightest heed, merely looking *bleak,* my dear, and then he whipped up his horses and off they flew, leaving Addison in the middle of a compliment. One can't think, *really,* why Rossiter ever offered for the girl, for it is quite clear that they will never suit; but she has got him, and I daresay she means to keep him. Quite penniless, one hears, and they say *he* is rich enough now to buy an Abbey—"

All this was of mixed comfort to Cressida, since no matter how satisfactory it might be to have her conviction confirmed that Rossiter did not care for Kitty, it was just as *un*satisfactory to reflect that there was no honourable way for him to cry off from his obligation to marry her, so long as Kitty chose to hold him to it. But she possessed her soul in tolerable patience until the Wednesday evening, when she, Kitty, and Lady Constance (the latter under protest, for she could never forget that Sir Octavius, in spite of his present eminence, had begun his career in a counting-house) drove to the elegant mansion in Pall Mall that was Sir Octavius's residence when he was in town.

Lady Constance, of course, had never entered that austerely gracious portal before, but Cressida could see that she was immediately struck by the luxury and taste that surrounded her as soon as she had stepped across the threshold. Sir Octavius, the friend and patron of most of the great figures in the London world of art and literature over the past thirty years, had been over that same period an amateur of the arts whose collection was the envy of the most knowledgeable connoisseurs in the kingdom. Chinese porcelains, French boiseries and tapestries, a rare red-figured Etruscan hydria, a mediaeval silver bowl ingeniously decorated with chased and engraved letters from the old black-letter alphabet, Flemish miniatures, Oriental japanned cabinets—each apartment contained something unusual and exquisite, displayed with unerring taste.

Cressida, who had dined at the house on several previous occasions, was quite prepared to be dazzled anew, but she saw Lady Constance's eyes narrow appreciatively as they took in the splendours that surrounded her—"*So* like the Single Cube Room at Wilton," she complimented the magnificent proportions of the drawing room, with its chimney-pieces of Italian marble, its ornate coved ceiling, and its exuberant display of carved and gilded wood—and even Kitty, whose idea of art did not go beyond the latest design for her tambour-work, was obviously overawed.

Perhaps fortunately for Cressida's self-composure, Rossiter had not yet put in an appearance before she and her party arrived, and they found only Captain Harries seated with their host. She was therefore able to greet Rossiter, when he did come in, from the advantageous position of being a member of a group, and was further buoyed up by seeing that, unlike her, he had obviously had no advance information as to whom he was to meet that evening.

This rather surprised her, as she had expected, as a matter of course, that Kitty would have told him; but she soon discovered that communication between the two betrothed lovers scarcely seemed to be of the sort to encourage confidences even of an ordinary social nature. They were placed side by side at dinner, but their conversation, from what Cressida could hear of it, consisted of the merest commonplaces, and each appeared relieved when able to turn to converse with the person upon his or her other side.

"They *can't* care a groat for each other!" Cressida thought, which reflection ought to have lifted her spirits considerably; but since Rossiter's manner towards *her* was so cool as to make his attitude towards Kitty seem, by contrast, positively ardent, she really found very little in the situation upon which to congratulate herself.

As was customary, Sir Octavius kept his gentlemen for some time in the dining room over their wine after the ladies had retired to the drawing room, during which period Cressida had ample opportunity to wonder what on earth he expected to accomplish from this extraordinarily dull and uncomfortable dinner-party. She also wondered whether she would have the opportunity to speak privately to Rossiter which Sir Octavius had apparently intended her to have, and, if so, what she would say to him.

Everything must depend, she felt, upon Rossiter's own attitude—and that that attitude had undergone a marked change for the worse, as far as she was concerned, during the period he had spent with Sir Octavius and Captain Harries in the dining room, was at once apparent when he entered the drawing room. Coolness seemed to have given way to a definite exasperation, and the look he bent upon her was so decidedly unfriendly that she hastily moved to a table at the other side of the room and picked up Pococke's *Description of the East*, which lay upon it.

But Sir Octavius, who could be as masterful when the situation demanded it as he could be subtle when subtlety was called for, soon put an end to this temporising.

"Now, Cressy, my dear," he said, firmly taking Mr. Pococke's volume from her and replacing it upon the table, "I shall show you my Egyptian Room. It is quite complete at all points now, and I know you will find it interesting. Come along." And, as she moved off obediently down the room with him, he went on, steering her over to the chaste Adam mantelpiece against which Rossiter was moodily leaning, "I shan't bore the others with it, but you, Rossiter"—drawing the unwilling Captain irresistibly into his orbit—"will enjoy having a look at it. My new Egyptian Room, that is." And he repeated, this time for the Captain's benefit, "Come along."

Unless Rossiter was prepared to be very rude indeed to his host and state firmly that he had not the least interest in seeing the Egyptian Room, there was nothing for it but for him to accompany Sir Octavius and Cressida across the broad hall to a small apartment decorated in the pale yellows and bluish greens, relieved by black and gold, which, as Sir Octavius kindly informed them, predominated among the pigments of ancient Egypt.

"You might note particularly the statue of Sen-Nefer," he remarked, as he led them into the room. "A very unusual piece, I believe. And now I must rejoin my other guests."

He went off with his blandest smile, leaving Cressida and Rossiter confronting each other before the massive granite figure to which he had referred. It was Rossiter who spoke first, with a slight, contemptuous curl of the lip.

"Transparent!" he said. "Is this your doing? But for what purpose? If it is to assure me that that little scene I witnessed that night at the Maybridges' leaves you entirely innocent of any designs upon Miles, Mayr has already contrived to drop a word in my ear to let me know how matters stand in that regard. And it is a pity," he went on in an even more savage tone, for quite evidently he had been driven to the very end of his patience by this evening of discomfort and sudden revelation, "that no one had the wit to inform me of Miles's attachment for Miss Chenevix before I offered for her myself! It had been *my* understanding that he was dangling after *you!*"

If Cressida had done what any intelligent young woman would have done, and what she had fully determined beforehand to do should any opportunity for such action present itself, she would have melted into tears, cast herself upon Rossiter's breast, and declared her own love for him in modest, though shaken, accents.

What she actually did, however, was to say with entire candour and considerable spirit that if he hadn't been a nodcock he would have been able to see for himself how matters stood. She then realised that she had said quite the wrong thing, and in an effort to retrieve her mistake began hastily to speak again, but was at once interrupted by Rossiter.

"How the devil," he demanded wrathfully, "was I to know how matters stood when Miles was underfoot in Mount Street every time I stepped inside your front door? And then to come upon him embracing you—"

"In a purely *brotherly* way," Cressida interjected with great hauteur, her chin well up in the air.

"Very well: in a *brotherly* way, if you insist! But

embracing you, all the same! If you weren't such a curst flirt—"

"I do *not* flirt! And especially not with someone like Miles. I *told* you I wouldn't!" said Cressida indignantly, rapidly finding the pose of aloof superiority she had adopted in her preceding speech quite inadequate for the occasion and descending to more earthbound levels.

"Exactly!" said Rossiter grimly. "You told me you wouldn't, and—the more fool I!—I believed you! Which is why, when I saw the two of you together at that damnable ball, I thought it must be serious and that you— that he—"

"Oh, Dev!" exclaimed Cressida, halfway between laughter and tears at this sudden revelation of the state of mind that had led to that abrupt proposal of marriage at the Maybridges' ball. "Do you mean you thought Miles and I were intending to marry and *that* was why you went and offered for Kitty in the middle of a set of country dances? But how *could* you? You *must* think me the most fickle creature alive, to be turning Langmere off in one breath and taking poor Miles on in the next!"

"I have good reason," said Rossiter scathingly, "to think you the most fickle creature alive, my girl! Since I have come back to London I have had nothing but tales of your conquests dinned into my ears—how you have had one poor devil after another dangling at your shoestrings, leading each of them up to the very brink of matrimony before you turn cat in pan and are off again after greener fields! But if you are thinking you have added me to your list, you are fair and far off! God knows, if I had had the slightest inkling that Miles had formed an attachment for Miss Chenevix, I should never have made her an offer myself; but if it hadn't been Miss Chenevix, I can assure you that it would have been any other female in London rather than you!" He broke off, regarding her now stormy face inimically, and then went on, between shut teeth, "What is it, exactly, that you want of me. Cressy? To prove to yourself that you can whistle me back whenever you wish, as you can all the others? Well, I will tell you now, there is not the least chance of that! I've no fancy to be made a bobbing-block for the whole town to snigger over, as Langmere was when you flung *him* off—"

"Oh!" gasped Cressida, who could contain herself no longer. "What a *contemptible* wretch you are! As if I *wished* to make Leonard unhappy, or ridiculous! *I* have been far more unhappy, I am sure, than he! But that, of course, is nothing to you! And if *I*," she went on, so full of rage and disappointment now that she could scarcely control her shaking voice, "am the last woman in London you would wish to offer for, you may be assured that *you* are the last man in London from whom I should accept an offer! Arrogant, disagreeable, unreasonable—I am sure I pity poor Kitty Chenevix from the bottom of my heart!"

She could not remain a moment longer, she felt, facing him before that great, serene statue, which had endured in its granite impassivity for thousands of years while lovers had quarrelled and broken their hearts and disappeared into the darkness of time past. She moved swiftly past him out of the room, pausing in the hall, beneath the equally impassive gaze of a liveried footman stationed beside the door, to dash the angry tears from her eyes before she re-entered the drawing room.

If she had not been so taken up with her own unhappy feelings, the tableau she saw before her as she came into the room might have given her a moment's astonished pause. Captain Harries and Kitty stood together at the far end of the room before a large, glass-fronted case containing a magnificent display of early seventeenth century Le Bourgeoys flintlocks, their stocks decorated with silver, mother-of-pearl, gilt brass, and carved ivory. These they appeared to be examining, although far more interested, it seemed, in their own conversation than in the display before them, while beside the fireplace Lady Constance and Sir Octavius sat together, deep in confidential talk. So absorbed were the latter two, in fact, that for a few moments neither of them was aware of Cressida's presence. What they could be finding to talk of, upon this their first meeting, that was of such great mutual interest Cressida could not imagine, but she distinctly overheard the words, "marriage settlements," uttered by Lady Constance as she trod across the carpet towards them, and she wondered bitterly if it were possible that even Sir Octavius had so far despaired of her cause, despite his own efforts in her behalf, that he was now discussing with Lady Constance the settlements that Rossiter would make upon Kitty when they were married.

Still there was, she considered in slight surprise as she sat down beside them, a distinctly startled, almost guilty, look upon Lady Constance's face as she looked up and saw her, which would scarcely have been the case had she merely been talking of Kitty, and even Sir Octavius's usual quizzical calm seemed to have deserted him momentarily. A certain unwonted air of satisfaction was evident in his manner, and there was a gleam in those ordinarily shrewdly veiled dark eyes which, men active upon 'Change might have informed her (some very ruefully), appeared there only when their owner had concluded a most advantageous bargain.

Cressida, however, was in no case to speculate upon the significance of these details, being fully occupied with her own harried emotions, which were divided at the moment between despair at her having thrown away her last chance to detach Rossiter from Kitty and a feeling of vengeful satisfaction at having at least given as good as she had got during the disagreeable scence that had just taken place in the Egyptian Room. Not even with the penalty of going through life with a permanently broken heart, she thought impenitently, would she had given up the satisfaction of rejecting him as rudely as he had rejected her. And this consideration was sufficient to carry her, with battle colours still flying, through the remainder of the evening, which fortunately was of no long duration, for Rossiter, upon returning to the drawing room, almost immediately took his departure.

This was the signal for Cressida to indicate a wish to do likewise, and, though Lady Constance showed a surprising unwillingness to leave so soon, and even Kitty, who was being consoled in the most agreeable manner for Rossiter's almost total neglect of her that evening by Captain Harries's modestly admiring attentions, seemed more eager to remain than to go, Cressida carried the day, and the carriage was sent for.

In the hall, as they were taking leave of their host, Sir Octavius took the opportunity to have a private word with her.

"I gather," he said, looking at her shrewdly, "my meddling was to no good effect?"

"None whatever," she said shortly, drawing on her gloves.

"A pity!" said Sir Otavius, and added enigmatically, "I should otherwise have considered this a most successful evening."

She glanced up at him in astonishment, but the carriage had been brought round and the others were already going out the door. There was nothing for her to do but to follow them, and so she did, but what possible sort of success Sir Octavius could have attributed to an evening that had been, so far as she had been able to see compounded merely of dullness and frustration, it was beyond her powers of imagination to conceive.

CHAPTER 14

The upshot of the evening, as far as she herself was concerned, was that it had ended as it had begun—with Rossiter as firmly betrothed to Kitty as ever, and with his still having not the least notion of the true state of her feelings towards him. The entire situation was, she considered, in a hopeless muddle, and so despondent was she over it that she almost wished that the letter that had been sent off to Kitty's mama in Devonshire, informing her of the splendid prospect before her daughter and requesting her blessing upon the engagement, might receive an affirmative reply the very next day, so that immediate arrangements might be made for the wedding.

"Once he is actually married, I daresay I shall be able to put him out of my mind quite easily," she told herself the next morning, with more bravado than conviction; and to prove to herself how little she really cared for the odious Captain, she accepted an invitation from a very dashing Polish count to drive out to the Botanical Gardens, where she flirted outrageously with him and promised him that he might escort her to the Venetian breakfast that was to be given at a great house in Chiswick the following day.

All of which in no way lifted the oppression of spirit that had lain so heavily upon her ever since the evening of the Maybridges' ball, and as she entered the front door of her house in Mount Street, after bidding farewell in her gayest voice to the Polish count, she was hoping devoutly that no one had, or would, come to call upon them, as what she would really like to do was to go upstairs to her own bedchamber and cry her eyes out.

Her wish was fulfilled to the extent that no sound of polite conversation reached her ears as she passed the drawing-room door, but she had not gone five paces past it before Lady Constance suddenly emerged from it and pounced upon her.

"Oh, Cressy, I am *so* glad you are come home!" she exclaimed, and Cressida saw with some surprise that her face wore an expression of highly affronted agitation upon it. "I have not the *least* notion what to do," she went on, "and there is that wretched girl upstairs pretending to be doing nothing more wicked than mending a rent in my puce satin gown, when all the while I *know* what is in her mind, and that she is merely *waiting* for this note to be brought to her!" And to Cressida's astonishment she thrust a crumpled sheet of notepaper into her hand, adding tragically, "I *knew*, of course, the moment I came upon Harbage with it a few minutes ago and he said Mr. Addison's groom had brought it by hand for Miss Chenevix, what it was! I think I must have had a premonition! So I said I would take it to her myself, and instead I opened it and read it—such a really *immoral* thing to do, I daresay, but then it would have been even *more* wicked to let her read it, when I *knew* it could mean nothing but mischief! It has all seemed *quite* too good to be true, you see—such a *very* advantageous offer, and in her first Season—and now she is going to throw it all away, and be ruined, besides, for Addison will *never* marry her, you know, no matter what he says!"

While this bewildering flood of word was being poured out, Cressida, according it only half her attention, was reading the few lines written in an elegant masculine hand on the sheet of notepaper that Lady Constance had given her.

My dearest love, the words ran, *I have completed the arrangements. You will meet me at the White Hart in Welwyn. As we planned, you must contrive an errand in Bond Street this afternoon with no one but Lady Con's maid accompanying you. Give her the slip, and the chaise will be waiting around the corner in Bruton Street. The off-leader will wear a white cockade. Don't give the game away by taking anything with you, and, if you love me, don't leave a note behind. Too, too bourgeois, my dear, and it will do Cressy and Lady Con a world of credit to have a genuine disappearance on their hands. One does so like to create a sensation in the middle of the Season, when everyone is* ennuyé *with balls and breakfasts.* A bientôt. *Your* most devoted *Addison.*

Cressida looked up in utter astonishment. "No, I *can't* believe it!" she said. "Kitty to be planning an elopement with Addison—and in broad daylight! She must be mad! They must both be mad! He cannot possibly wish to marry her—"

"Oh, no! I am *quite* persuaded that he does not!" Lady Constance distractedly agreed. "But no doubt he has cozened her into *believing* that he does. This talk of meeting her in Welwyn—of course it will appear to *her* that he intends taking her north to the Border—but can you imagine Addison, of all men, planning to be married in Gretna over the anvil? It is perfectly plain that he means merely to ruin the girl, in order to revenge himself upon Rossiter."

Cressida, who had grown a trifle paler but was now quite in command of herself, continued to stare fixedly down at the note in her hand.

"But can he really have considered the consequences?" she said after a moment, more to herself, it seemed, than to Lady Constance. "If he *does* ruin Kitty, Rossiter will be certain to call him out—"

"Oh, my dear, I daresay he does not care for that!" Lady Constance said. "He is held to be an excellent shot, I have always heard it said, and you know he has been out more than once—that affair of poor young Worthington, for example." She shrugged her shoulders with an air of meaningful cynicism. "My dear papa was always used to say," she observed trenchantly, "that when a man's lower nature was aroused, he feared *nothing,* and I believe that is exactly the state Addison is in, or he would never have concocted such a monstrous scheme! But what are we to *do* to stop him?"

Cressida, becoming conscious at this moment of the impropriety of their continuing the conversation where any passing servant might overhear them, led her into the drawing room and closed the door.

"Do?" she said then, slowly. "Why, we might lock her in her room, I daresay—that would scotch the plan for today, at least. But we most certainly cannot keep her there indefinitely, and if she remains in London he may very easily contrive to see her again and make other plans for eloping with her. He has enough gall to do so even if we confront him with this note! And we *can't* tell Rossiter of it: that *would* throw the fat in the fire! He would be quite certain to call Addison out—"

"And then there would be a scandal, and no doubt he wouldn't marry Kitty, after all!" Lady Constance said, sinking down upon an ivory satinwood sofa with a tragical expression upon her face. "Oh, dear! Oh, dear! That wretched, idiotish girl! She has always seemed so *very* sensible—and then to do such a wicked, foolish thing as this, just when she is on the verge of being settled so prosperously!"

"She doesn't care for him, you know," Cressida said, standing very erect and still in the centre of the room, her face quite expressionless. "I daresay, if the truth were told, she doesn't care for either of them—only she is frightened of Dev, and dazzled by Addison. To be the chosen bride of the *premier dandy* in London—" She made a sudden gesture of violent impatience. "Good God, is she really so enamoured of herself as to believe that a poor little dab of a girl like her can have penetrated the armour of that man's indifference and pride?" she exclaimed. "It would take a Royal princess to accomplish that! But we must not stand here doing nothing! We must have some sort of plan, or heaven knows what will come of all this!"

She sank down into the chair that stood before an elegant little French writing-desk and, spreading Addison's note out before her, mechanically read it through again, as if hoping against hope that there might be something in it to cause her to believe that the meaning she and Lady Constance had seen in it might be in error. But the significance was only too clear: Addison certainly meant to ruin Kitty, and Cressida believed him to be quite capable of accomplishing this purpose even if she and Lady Constance were immediately to bundle the girl out of London, back to her home in Devonshire. One could run away from Devonshire quite as well as one could from London; and then there was the fact that the taking of any drastic precautions to protect Kitty from her would-be seducer must necessarily defeat what was, to Cressida at least, their primary purpose—that of keeping Rossiter in the dark as to Addison's intentions.

For if he were to guess at Addison's purpose, he would—he must—call him out, and, confident as she was of Rossiter's ability to drop his opponent, she could in no wise be certain that Addison—also a splendid marksman, as Lady Constance had reminded her—

would not likewise be able to hit his mark. She had pooh-poohed the idea of a duel when Lady Dalingridge had broached the matter to her a few days before, not believing for a moment that Addison was willing to advertise to the world, by calling Rossiter out, his pique over the latter's having carried Kitty off in spite of his own marked attentions to her.

But she was well aware that Addison was no coward, and the prospect of having Rossiter, in the role of the gulled betrothed, call *him* out would certainly add the final fillip to his triumph.

"I *must* find *some* way to prevent all this!" she thought in despair. "If only I could contrive somehow to make *him* appear a figure of ridicule! It is the only thing that will put an end to this horrid plan, for he is vulnerable nowhere but in his vanity!"

Lady Constance's voice came across the room to her in a kind of low wail.

"Oh, what *are* we to do? I feel myself so responsible! After all, the child *did* put herself so *trustingly* into our care! And now we have led her into *this!*"

"Nonsense!" said Cressida, her exasperation boiling over at this quite unwarranted aspersion upon herself and Lady Constance. "We have led her into nothing; it is all her own folly and ambition. If she had not foisted the most barefaced untruth upon us by giving us to understand that her aunt was too ill to bring her out, she would never have come near Mount Street, and would have spent the Season with a set of comfortable, worthy nobodies—which would not have suited her in the least, you know! All the same, we can't let the wretched girl ruin herself! We shall be obliged to do *something*, if only to see to it that Rossiter is not killed on the head of it!"

Lady Constance, her attention momentarily diverted from the problem before her, stared at her.

"But what can you mean, my love?" she demanded.

"A barefaced untruth—?"

"Yes!" said Cressida. "There has been, and is, nothing in the world wrong with Mrs. Mills's health. I met her at Mrs. Torrance's in Keppel Street not a week after Kitty came to us, and she told me herself that she had not been ill. Of course she had not the least notion that Kitty had alleged *that* as her reason for wishing to come to us; she merely thought it had been all our kindness in inviting her. No," she went on, as Lady Constance opened her mouth to speak, "I didn't disillusion her. I only wish now that I had done, and then sent Kitty packing back to Devonshire. *That* has been *my* only fault in this affair!"

She arose and began pacing impatiently up and down the long room. They would have to come to some decision soon, she felt, for Kitty must already be growing uneasy upstairs as the note she had been expecting failed to arrive, and they had no way of knowing what imprudences she might be led into, in her anxiety not to fail in arriving at the chosen rendezvous. Addision had used the words, "as we planned," so that it was obvious the matter had been discussed by them previously, and Kitty might well be aware of the chaise even now awaiting her arrival in Bruton Street. She would have only to slip out of the house and walk to the fatal corner, and she would be whisked away to her meeting with Addison in Welwyn.

And if someone else were to go in her place? the thought suddenly came into Cressida's mind. If Addison were to find, as he stepped forward to hand a blushing and inexperienced girl from the chaise in the inn-yard of the White Hart, that what he had got instead was the dashing Miss Calverton, armed with cool sarcasms and fully prepared to spread the tale of his discomfiture all over London—?

"I have it!" she announced triumphantly. "The very

thing! *I* shall go in Kitty's place!"

Lady Constance, who was still mulling Kitty's duplicity in the matter of Mrs. Mills indignantly over in her mind, looked at her mistrustfully.

"What did you say, dear?" she enquired.

"I said, I shall go in her place!" Cressida repeated impatiently, making for the door.

Lady Constance gave a faint shriek.

"Now, don't, pray *don't* fly up into the boughs!" Cressida admonished her, pausing to give her a bracing hug. "I promise you, I shall be *quite* all right, but I intend to give Mr. Drew Addison the shock of his life! I daresay he will not try a second time to elope with Kitty when he realises *I* have the power to let everyone in London into the jest of his having laid the most elaborate plans to carry off *one* young lady, only to find that he had actually got quite another, who had not the least intention of becoming his innocent victim! And everyone in London *shall* know of it, if I do not receive his most solemn assurance that he will never attempt anything of the sort again! Dear ma'am, pray *don't* try to stop me," she added, as Lady Constance, almost overcome with incredulous astonishment and disapproval, again began uttering objections, "for I have quite made up my mind to go! Only let me put on a close bonnet that will hide my face—though I am sure the postillions who are waiting with the chaise in Bruton Street are hired, and have no notion what Kitty looks like—and I shall be off!"

She sped out of the room, giving Lady Constance a last reassuring hug, and in the hall directed Harbage to have the barouche brought round at once. Ten minutes later, having made a rapid change into a demure blue gown of French cambric, and with a large Pamela bonnet concealing her tawny curls and the greater part of her face, she was seating in her carriage on her way to Bond Street, having left Lady Constance almost distracted in the drawing room, with her vinaigrette close at hand, and quite certain that this fateful day would not come to an end before she had seen the utter ruin of one or both of the young ladies now under her charge.

As for Cressida herself, she had no such premonitions. She would go to Welwyn, confront Addison, and return to Mount Street, where she would inform Kitty in no uncertain terms of the fate she had escaped, and attempt to drum some modicum of sense into her head on the subject of men like Addison, who cared more for their own vanity than they would ever do for any woman. In the case of this latter project she was not overly sanguine of success, for young ladies who had allowed *their* vanity to lead them to the point of throwing their cap over the windmill, in the belief that their cleverness would bring them about in the end , were not, in her experience, apt to abandon their golden dreams without a struggle.

Still, if Addison, for his part, were now to quit his pursuit of her, there was very little she could do but abandon those dreams, and settle instead for the reality within her grasp—namely, marriage to Rossiter. It was this thought—that, by saving Kitty from Addison, she was undoubtedly giving up her last opportunity to see the engagement between her and Rossiter broken off— that had caused Cressida, as she had been changing her dress in her bedchamber a few minutes before, almost to falter in her purpose and to let matters take their course as far as Addison and Kitty were concerned.

But a moment's reflection had stiffened her resolution. She *could not* see Rossiter placed in a position in which he would feel obliged to call Addison out; neither could she allow a girl who was under her protection to be ruined without making a push to prevent it.

So she had gone on with her preparations, and now,

arriving in Bond Street, she ordered her coachman to halt the carriage and, having alighted from it, dismissed him, sending him back to Mount Street. A few minutes' walk then brought her to Bruton Street, and the first thing she saw, when she turned the corner, was a yellow-bodied chaise-and-four standing beside the flagway, its off-leader sporting a white cockade.

She approached it, counterfeiting—rather well, she prided herself—timidity and agitation in her demeanour. One of the postillions, observing her, jumped down, opened the door of the chaise, and stood waiting for her to enter. She did so, once more pretending an uncertainty she did not in the least feel, and in a few moments the door had been closed behind her, the postillion had again sprung upon his mount, and the chaise was rattling off quickly through the crowded London streets.

Cressida sat back comfortably against the cushions and folded her hands composedly in her lap.

"And now, Mr. Addison," she said to herself, with a light in her eye that boded ill for that gentleman when they met, "and *now* we shall see which is the dupe—the young lady you have persuaded to meet you at the White Hart in Welwyn, or yourself!"

CHAPTER 15

To Cressida, impatient for her encounter with Addison, the journey to Welwyn seemed interminable, though the postillions, who were evidently under orders to make their best speed to the rendezvous, kept their horses at the gallop and forebore to take the time for a change at Barnet.

It was therefore not much past seven when they swept into the inn-yard of the White Hart. As they rattled to a halt, Cressida looked out the window of the chaise to see if Addison had been on the watch for it, but he was nowhere in sight. Raising her brows at this lack of ardour —for in the interest of accomplishing a successful seduction he might at least, she felt, have pretended to an impatience he did not feel—she was gathering up her skirts, preparatory to alighting from the chaise, when to her surprise one of its doors abruptly opened and a very large, heavy-set man in a green coat stepped in and sat down beside her. At the same moment she became aware that the postillions had jumped down from their mounts and were apparently engaged in urgently speeding the efforts of a pair of ostlers to put-to a fresh team.

"What—?" she began in astonished indignation, but the heavy-set man interrupted her at once.

"Never fear, miss!" he said, in what she supposed was meant to be an ingratiating manner, although the low accent and the meaningful leer upon his broad, mis-shapen features were far from reassuring to her. "All's bowman. The master sent me to see you safe to the end of your journey."

"To the end of my journey! But—you can't mean, to Scotland!" ejaculated Cressida, wondering for a rather disagreeable moment if the man was mad, and making an effort to free herself from the large hand that had clamped itself heavily upon her arm as she made a motion as if to leave the chaise by the other door.

The man chuckled. "Nay, it's not so far as *that*," he said. "A matter of half a dozen miles, is all. And you'll find the master waiting for you there."

"I wish," said Cressida wrathfully, "you will remove your hand from my arm, sir. I should like to leave the chaise—"

"Nay, nay—master wouldn't like that!" the man said, growing more serious as her struggle to free her arm from his grasp intensified. "You're to come straight along with me, miss. *That's* what he said."

"If you do not let me go," she said fiercely, "I shall scream!"—and found herself dragged back on the instant against the cushions, one heavy hand clapped over her mouth, while with the other she was held firmly against a mountainous and muscular chest. At the same moment the ostlers, who, urged on by the postillions, had made good their employer's boast that a change could be made in no more than ninety seconds at his inn, sprang away from the horses' heads and the chaise went rattling brisk-ly out of the inn-yard to the road beyond.

Once they had passed the environs of Welwyn and the chaise was bowling rapidly along the high road again,

Cressida found herself abruptly released and her companion grinning over sheepishly at her.

"I couldn't help it, missy," he said to her apologetically. "The master said I was to bring you straight away—"

"The master! The master! Who *is* your master?" Cressida sputtered, attempting to set her bonnet, which had been pushed sadly awry by the mauling she had received, at a more seemly angle upon her head.

The man looked at her in surprise. "Why, Mr. Addison, to be sure," he said. "Beant you love-shotten with him, and he waiting to greet you at the house?"

"Addison!" Cressida caught her breath. So the man was not mad, and had been sent by Addison to escort her —where? To "the house," he had said, and she remembered suddenly that Addison indeed possessed a hunting-box in this vicinity.

It was his intention, then, she could only suppose, to accomplish Kitty's seduction there; and for some reason the thought of facing him upon his own grounds, in an isolated country house with only his own servants about—and probably not even many of them, since he was not in residence there at this time—was far less agreeable to her than the idea had been of confronting him in a public inn, with dozens of other persons about and help at hand at any moment if she should require it.

There was nothing for it, however, but to brazen the matter through, for quite obviously there was no way in which she could now avoid that meeting with him. She accordingly leaned back with what composure she could against the cushions and tried to think what she would say, which was fatal. The more she thought of the approaching scene, the more convinced she became that she had chosen quite the wrong way in which to handle the matter, and her only consolation was that, if she had had an extremely unpleasant shock in finding herself being carried off against her will from the yard of the White Hart, Addison was certainly going to face one equally disagreeable when his henchman delivered her, and not Kitty, into his clutches.

She had not long to wait before that moment arrived, for, as the man in the green coat had predicted, the chaise had gone less than half a dozen miles when it turned off the high road into a rough lane, over which it jolted uncomfortably for several minutes before arriving at a pair of lodge gates, whence a short drive led to a house set about so thickly with trees that it was almost invisible from the lane.

Up this drive the horses were now turned; the chaise came to a halt before the front door of the house; the man in the green coat jumped out; and Cressida, rejecting as useless the idea of bribing the postillions to whip up their horses and drive her back to the White Hart, found herself assisted by the man in the green coat to alight. With one hand tightly clasping her arm he then urged her up the steps to the door, which was immediately opened for them by a person—she could not think him a butler—quite as villainous-looking as her companion, who tipped the latter a wink, gave her a broad leer, and then jerked his head in the direction of a door opening on the left of the hall.

"In there," he said; and without more ado the man in the green coat, still grasping her firmly by the arm, brought her across the hall and through the open door into a comfortable library, where Addison sat at his ease, perusing the latest copy of the *Racing Chronicle*.

At the sound of their footsteps he glanced up, putting aside his journal with a lazy, prepared smile upon his lips. But the next moment that smile had disappeared abruptly from his face, to be replaced by an expression (alas for his vaunted reputation of never allowing any event, no matter how disturbing or unusual, to overset the bored calm of his manner!) of utter astonishment.

"You!" he ejaculated, in an incredulous and, indeed, quite stupefied tone. "But—but where is—?"

"Where is Kitty?" she finished it for him coolly, her spirits rising rapidly at the sight of his discomfiture. She trod further into the room, freed now from the grasp of the green-coated man, who had prudently retreated into the hall, and confronted him with a slight and, she hoped, convincingly mocking smile. "My dear man, did you really believe that Lady Con and I look after her so poorly that she could go jauntering off in post-chaises without our being aware of it?" she continued. "What an innocent you are, after all! You have been bubbled, you see! Kitty, unfortunately for you, is safe in Mount Street, and, even more unfortunately, you, I fear, will soon be the laughingstock of London! A totally ridiculous situation to find yourself in—is it not?—having laid such elaborate plans to lure Kitty into your net, and then finding I am come instead! I am sure all our friends will be highly diverted when I tell the tale to them!"

She paused, glancing at him interrogatively for response to this sally; but what she saw made her take an involuntary step backward, and the smile suddenly faded from her lips. She had seen men in a fury before, but never one from whose eyes there blazed such malignant hatred that she felt it ought to have scorched her where she stood.

It was at that moment that she became aware that the house was very still, and it was borne in upon her forcibly that in all probability the rogue who had brought her there and the one who had met them at the door were its only occupants, beyond Addison and herself. She was no coward, but the alarming conviction abruptly began to grow upon her that, in taking Kitty's place in that post-chaise waiting in Bruton Street, she had done something not only foolhardy but decidedly dangerous as well.

Somewhat to her surprise, however, Addison,

instead of rounding upon her in violent terms, or doing even worse, merely turned his back upon her and, walking away from her across the room, took up a decanter that stood upon a tray on a table. Splashing some of its contents into a glass, he set it down and raised the glass to his lips; then he put the glass down as well and turned to her again.

"Remiss of me!" he said, in a dry, grim voice. "Would you care to join me in a glass of madeira, my dear?"

"No, thank you!" said Cressida, very much relieved to find that the social amenities were still to be observed between them. "In point of fact," she went on, "I should like nothing more than the use of a carriage and horses to take me back to the White Hart at once. It is growing late, and I dislike travelling in the dark."

Addison, who had again raised his glass to his lips upon her refusal of the wine, drank off its contents deliberately before he set it down once more upon the table.

"As to that," he said then, in the same carefully controlled voice, "you need be under no apprehension, my dear Cressy. You will not be travelling to Welwyn or anywhere else until it is full light again. In short," he continued, regarding her fixedly, with a slight, disagreeable smile upon his lips, as she made a gesture of incomprehension, "you are spending the night here, my love. After all, it is only fair play—is it not? You wished to take Kitty's place. Very well: you may take it. May I suggest that you now remove your bonnet and make yourself comfortable? You must be hungry after your journey, and there is an excellent cold collation laid out in the dining room."

Cressida had frequently read the words in romantic novels, *His (or her) blood ran cold,* but she had never before experienced the peculiar sensation thus described, and had been rather inclined to believe that no such sensation existed in real life.

She now realised her error. Her blood might not actually have become appreciably chilled in her veins at that moment, but she most certainly felt as if it had, and it was not at all an agreeable feeling. If it was now Addison's intention to accomplish *her* ruin instead of Kitty's, she realised, she was in a most precarious situation. The house was an isolated one; the servants—probably hired for the occasion out of some low tavern in Tothill Fields—would assuredly do nothing to thwart their master's intentions; and she was utterly without means to summon anyone else to her aid. Her only recourse, she saw, lay in her tongue, and she now summoned up all her wit to make use of it to good purpose.

"Don't, pray, be absurd, Drew!" she said to him in her most bored London drawing-room manner. "You must know I have not the least taste for melodramatic games! I shan't deny that your cold collation tempts me, but I am sure the White Hart sets a very good table, and I am persuaded that I shall arrive there in half an hour behind any horses you have in *your* stables—"

"My dear Cressy, you mistake me." Addison, well in control of himself now, spoke evenly, but there was still a dangerous glitter in those cold grey eyes. "I am playing no game—or, if I am, it is one that you have begun yourself. It will desolate me, I assure you, if you have no taste for finishing it, but, really, my dear, that scarcely signifies now. There is only one way, you see, in which I can be sure that you will remain silent on the subject of this disagreeable little incident and that is by making quite certain that it will be no more to your advantage than to mine to bring it up in Polite Society. I do not think, dearest Cressy, that you will greatly care to publish the tale of *my* discomfiture when I am able to cap it with a charming story of my own of how you spent the

night here with me, and departed in the morning with—
shall we say?—your virtue slightly more tarnished than
it was when you arrived."

He paused, gazing at her with an expression of
smug, expectant satisfaction upon his face. Cressida, her
lips compressed, merely regarded him warily. It was
clear to her now that the tack upon which she had begun
would accomplish nothing: Addison, having hit upon
what was—she was obliged to admit—an infallible
scheme for ensuring her silence, was certainly not to be
discountenanced or shamed into letting his advantage
slip through his fingers.

But would he really, she asked herself almost incredulously, carry through such a cruel and entirely
despicable plan merely to save himself from embarrassment? She remembered Dolly Dalingridge's relation of
Prince Pückler-Muskau's appalled comments on the
utter vindictiveness of an English dandy faced with
social obloquy—unjust, to be sure, when applied to a
good-humoured man like Alvanley, unlikely even in a
Brummell, who could be ruthless but also had a kind of
cold, intact pride that would have made him turn in dis-
gust from such a revenge as this.

But Addison—Addison, she decided, looking into
that handsome, self-satisfied face with a clarity of per-
ception that was heightened by her danger, was capable
of doing exactly what he had threatened. To a man who
prized his position in Society as highly as he did, ridicule
was a kind of death, and to free himself from that fate he
would undoubtedly go to almost any length. The fact
that she despised him, and had for years been at few
pains to hide it, would merely lend spice to his conquest.

She made a sudden entirely instinctive decision,
turned round, and ran to the door.

It opened at once as she turned the knob, but as she
rushed through it she found herself confronting a large

and very solid obstacle—the man in the green coat.

"Tomkins!" said Addison's voice at the same moment imperatively behind her; and before the word was out of his mouth a heavy hand was clapped upon her arm. Simultaneously she saw that the outer door was still guarded by the same ruffian who had admitted her a few minutes before: obviously, it was futile for her to make any further attempt to escape.

She turned coldly upon Addison. "You *are*," she pronounced very clearly, "a perfect toad, Addison: quite how perfect I never until this moment knew. Shall we go in to supper? At least if I am obliged to endure your company, I need not do it in a famished condition."

Addison grinned at her unpleasantly.

"By all means, my dear," he said to her, and led the way into the dining room.

C H A P T E R   16

At about the time that Cressida had stepped into the post-chaise awaiting her—or, rather, Kitty—in Bruton Street, the knocker of her house in Mount Street sounded and Harbage, treading in a stately manner to the front door, admitted Captain Rossiter.

"Is Miss Chenevix at home?" the Captain demanded.

Harbage, noting without the slightest change in countenance that the caller's own face wore an expression little calculated to bring joy to the heart of his betrothed, said he fancied Miss Chenevix was with her ladyship at present, and if the Captain would care to wait in the Small Saloon while he ascertained—

"Thank you; there's no need for that. In the drawing room, are they? I'll go up," said the Captain, who was never one, as Harbage confided later to the housekeeper, to stand upon ceremony, although in this instance he, Harbage, would have thought it very much better if he had done so, as, from what he had heard a few moments before, passing the drawing-room door "quite by accident, of course," her ladyship was in the act of giving Miss Kitty a regular bear-garden jaw there, and it was a guinea to a gooseberry that Miss Kitty, who was already crying, would be having hysterics in a brace of snaps.

All of which, of course, Rossiter was quite unaware of as he walked upstairs and into the drawing room, but his intrusion was greeted with such an aghast stare on Lady Constance's part and such a burst of sobbing on Kitty's that he must indeed have been dull of comprehension if he had not understood at once that he had inadvertently stumbled upon a scene of embarrassing proportions that was taking place between them.

He checked upon the threshold, an expression of distaste upon his dark face.

"I beg your pardon," he said shortly. "It appears I have come at an inopportune time."

"Well, yes; in point of fact, you *have*, rather," said Lady Constance, distractedly. "I am afraid Kitty is not *quite* herself at the moment." She bent a severely minatory gaze upon her weeping protégée. "Kitty, dear, *do* endeavour to compose yourself and make your apologies to Captain Rossiter!" she said. "Your behaviour is not at all becoming!"

Kitty, however, who had just undergone the shock of being told by Lady Constance, under the stress of Cressida's departure, that All Had Been Discovered and that she was the wickedest, most ungrateful girl in Christendom, had succumbed to the welter of feelings of shame, fear, disappointment, and obstinacy that had not unnaturally overwhelmed her upon this disclosure, and only sobbed harder than ever.

"I had best leave, I daresay," said Rossiter, casting a glance upon his betrothed that left little doubt that he found the discovery that a young lady he had considered a model of quiet composure could become an unmanageable watering-pot a far from agreeable one. "My apologies, Lady Constance—"

Lady Constance, obviously relieved to hear this

speech, said immediately that it might, indeed, be best if he allowed poor Kitty a little time in which to compose herself.

"A letter from her mama," she said, improvising rapidly and inventively. "Or not precisely *from* her mama, but *concerning* her mama, for she is too ill, it appears, to write herself. Such a shock for dear Kitty!"

Rossiter said, in conventional sympathy, that he was very sorry, and was turning to leave when Kitty, with the inability of all reserved and self-contained natures, once they are fairly launched upon a dramatic scene, to know where to leave off, suddenly ceased sobbing and said, "Stop!"

Rossiter stopped.

"I want you to know," said Kitty, her voice still impeded by sobs and her bosom swelling, "that I shall never, *never* marry you! I love—"

"Kitty, be silent!" said Lady Constance awfully.

Kitty looked at her rebelliously. "I shan't!" she said. "You may have stopped me for today, but I shall never marry anyone but—"

"You will go to your room at once, you wicked, wicked girl!" Lady Constance interrupted hastily, seeing the results of weeks of effort flying out the window. She turned a conciliatory smile upon Rossiter. "The poor child is quite beside herself!" she said. "She does not in the least know what she is saying!"

Rossiter regarded her coolly.

"On the contrary," he said, "it appears to me that she knows precisely what she is saying, and that it may be a great deal better for both of us if she is given an opportunity to say it." He walked over to Kitty and stood before her. "What is it?" he asked her, not ungently. "You would like to be released from this engagement of ours—is that it?"

"Yes!" said Kitty, at the same moment that Lady

Constance very emphatically said, "No!" The latter continued, in a tone of dramatic appeal, "Captain Rossiter, you *won't* listen to what the child says when she is so upset—"

"I am not so upset that I don't know it is not Captain Rossiter, but Mr. Addison, whom I wish to marry!" Kitty said, an equal amount of drama in her own tones. She looked defiantly at Lady Constance. "You can't stop me, ma'am; indeed, there is no reason for anyone to try to do so!" she said. "Mr. Addison is a gentleman of good family —with an *excellent* position in Society—and *very* agreeable manners—besides being in love with me—*and*," she added with a baldness born of her frustration and excitement, "he is *quite* as rich as Captain Rossiter—"

Lady Constance threw up her hands. "Oh, *do* be quiet, you wretched girl!" she commanded, quite in desspair over this unlucky turn of events. She turned again to Rossiter. "Captain Rossiter, *indeed* you must not refine too much upon what the child says!" she adjured him. "She is so *very* young and inexperienced, and that *heartless* man has merely been toying with her affections, of course, without the least intention of anything serious coming of it—"

"He is *not* toying with my affections!" Kitty said angrily. "I should be on my way to marry him at this very moment if it were not for *your* interference!"

Rossiter looked, with what Lady Constance—whose own face was expressing consternation of the wildest sort —considered a most extraordinary lack of perturbation, into the defiant and mulish countenance of his betrothed.

"Do you know," he said mildly, "I believe I had best sit down and hear the whole of this. So you were planning on marrying Addison today, Miss Chenevix? May I enquire why I—as a presumably more or less interested party—was not informed of this decision upon your part?"

Kitty cast a scared glance at him, and after a moment, instead of replying, burst into tears again.

"For God's sake, don't do that!" commanded Rossiter in exasperation, his equanimity apparently more disturbed by her lack of self-control than by the fact that she had been planning shamelessly to jilt him. "If you think I am not as quite aware as you are that our engagement has been a mistake from the beginning, you must take me for a bottlehead, for nothing has been more apparent! But why, in the name of Jupiter, couldn't you have come to me frankly and told me that you wished to be free of it—?"

"But she *doesn't* wish to be free of it!" Lady Constance babbled, still clinging desperately to the hope that something might yet be salvaged from the wreck Kitty appeared to be bent upon making of her prospects. "Captain Rossiter, *do* go away and allow the child time to recover herself! She does not know in the least what she is saying!"

But Kitty, who had by this time got the bit well between her teeth, was heard at this point to say distinctly, overriding Lady Constance's efforts to continue speaking, that she knew exactly what she was saying and that she was going at once to Welwyn, no matter who tried to stop her. She further added that she considered Miss Calverton's action in going in her stead a piece of the most underhanded double-dealing she had ever heard of, and was beginning on a dark insinuation that Cressida's reasons for doing so had more to do with her own interest in Addison than with any altruistic desire to save Kitty from a disastrous mistake when Rossiter's voice cut sharply through her words.

"Miss Calverton?" he ejaculated. "What has *she* to do in the matter?"

He looked interrogatively and imperatively at Lady Constance. Lady Constance made for a moment as if to deny that she knew anything at all about it, but then gave it up with a gesture of futility.

"She has gone to Welwyn to meet Addison in Kitty's place, you see," she quavered, looking more than a little frightened herself as Rossiter's gaze appeared to her to darken more menacingly with each word she spoke. "Indeed, I could not stop her!" she defended herself. "She was *quite* determined—"

"Quite determined—yes, I can believe that!" Rossiter said savagely. "A more meddlesome, jingle-brained—" He broke off, rising abruptly. "And what did she hope to gain by this piece of quixotic nonsense?" he enquired, standing grimly before Lady Constance's chair. "Even *she* is not tottyheaded enough, I suppose, to imagine that she can appeal to Addison's better nature—?"

"No, no! It is not that at all!" Lady Constance assured him unhappily. "Her opinion of Addison is *quite* the same as yours and mine! But she is persuaded, you see, that nothing will do to make him give over his pursuit of Kitty but to cause him to appear in an odiously ridiculous light—" She broke off, suddenly regaining spirit under his accusing gaze. "Well, I could not help it!" she said with some acerbity. "You *know* what she is! It was like trying to stop a—a whirlwind!"

He gave an exasperated shrug. "Yes, I can readily imagine!" he was obliged to agree. "I have had experience of her! Well, she won't thank me for meddling, I daresay, but obviously someone must, and as I can see no one else cast in the role of her deliverer, I shall go to Welwyn myself. Did it never occur to her that under such circumstances a man like Addison might well be dangerous—?"

He broke off suddenly as Kitty, with a shriek of alarm, jumped up from her place and flung herself between him and the door.

"No, no!" she panted. "You shan't go! You mustn't! Oh, Captain Rossiter, for *my* sake—"

"What the devil is the matter with the girl?" demanded Rossiter, whose temper, never of the mildest, appeared to be in danger of slipping its leash entirely at this fresh outburst from his late betrothed. "Why shouldn't I go to Welwyn?"

"She thinks, of course," said Lady Constance severely, "that you intend calling Addison out, Captain Rossiter. I can only hope that no such wicked thought has crossed your mind! It would be quite disastrous to everyone concerned!"

"Disastrous to Addison, I daresay, if I should do so," Rossiter said grimly, "but I shan't! You are quite welcome to him, Miss Chenevix—that is, if he cares to have you, which, you will forgive me for saying, I am strongly inclined to doubt! You have made your choice, however, which leaves me free to make mine as well." He turned to Lady Constance. "Where in Welwyn may I expect to come up with this precious pair?" he demanded. "At one of the inns?"

"Yes—at the White Hart." Lady Constance, who appeared at length to have become convinced that any further efforts on her part to repair the tatters into which the engagement between him and Kitty had been rent were in vain, looked up at the Captain gloomily. "Addison had a post-chaise waiting in Bruton Street to take her—or, that is, Kitty—up and bring her there, where he was to meet her. It is not above half an hour since she left the house, so I daresay you may even come up with her on the road if you are driving those splendid Welsh-bred greys of yours. But what you are to say to her when you *do*," she added in a sudden renewal of agitation, "I am sure I cannot imagine! She will probably be *quite* angry with you for trying to stop her—"

"I expect she will be," Rossiter said coolly. "I shall see her safe home, all the same, whatever tempests she may choose to raise!"

"I daresay," said Lady Constance, who had been

doing some rapid calculating in her own head during this brief speech, and had come to the conclusion that, with Kitty's cause irretrievably lost, she had as well do a quick reverse and come down in Cressida's behalf, "I daresay I have no right to tell you this—"

"Then don't," recommended Rossiter, making for the door.

"—but I shall," continued Lady Constance, unperturbed. "She is in love with you, you know."

"She? Who?" Rossiter wheeled about abruptly, a thunderstruck expression upon his face. "You can't mean—"

"Cressy? But I *do*," said Lady Constance earnestly. "Oh, I know it seems *most* unlikely, for she is forever breaking squares with you, but it is true. She told me so herself, on the evening you and Kitty became engaged— not in so many words, of course, but anyone could see how unhappy she was, and when I charged her with it she would only say that it didn't signify. But it does, of course, if she is truly attached to you, which seems to me *quite* extraordinary, but, after all, one has known of stranger cases—"

Rossiter, ignoring these oblique aspersions cast upon his desirability as a lover and husband, here interrupted to enquire rather caustically whether Lady Constance's opinion of Cressida's present feelings towards him was based merely upon this highly inconclusive piece of evidence.

"No, it is not," said Lady Constance with dignity. "That is," she acknowledged, "it *was*, until today, but I have had a letter in this morning's post from Lady Letitia Conway–" She broke off, looking interrogatively at him. "You are acquainted with her, I think?"

"I am," said Rossiter briefly. "Well? Go on."

"Well, it is really a most extraordinary letter," Lady Constance said confidentially, "and I am not *quite* sure what to make of it, for dear Letty is so *oblique,* you know. But I *think* she means to tell me that she has come to the conclusion that Cressida has *really* been attached to you all these years, only she was under the impression that *you* did not care for *her* because of your having broken off your engagement to her—"

"I didn't break it off," interrupted Rossiter, "but I won't say I didn't make it damnably easy for her to do so! But go on," he commanded once more.

"Well, it *seems,*" said Lady Constance, who, with her usual volatility, had momentarily forgotten Kitty's predicament in her interest in this new topic of conversation, "that Letty happened to mention to dear Cressida an interview she had had with you at that time, upon which Cressida became *quite* agitated and let fall certain remarks that made Letty consider that she now saw the whole matter—I mean of your having wished to break off the engagement—in an entirely new light—"

She paused, looking inquisitively and knowledgeably at Rossiter, in whose countenance a dark flush had begun to rise.

"I believe," she went on after a moment, in a satisfied tone, "*she*—that is, Letty—believes that *she*—that is, Cressy—now considers your actions at that time as having been induced by the noblest motives—though I must say it appears to me that *any* gentleman worthy of the name, when faced with the fact that the young lady he is betrothed to stands to lose a fortune by marrying him, would at once withdraw his suit—"

But at this point Kitty, who, like all selfish people, took not the least interest in matters that did not appear likely to afford her any advantage, and was still full of rage and chagrin over her own thwarted opportunities, burst in upon the conversation once more to demand that Rossiter, if he indeed intended to drive to Welwyn, at least take her with him.

Lady Constance turned a scandalised face upon her.

"Take you with him!" she exclaimed. "Have you *no* sense of propriety, child!—asking the man you have jilted to take you to an assignation with the man you have jilted him for! Unheard of! *Quite* unheard of!"

Rossiter, who appeared all at once to have forgotten his irritation and instead seemed to have fallen into an extraordinarily good temper, grinned.

"Unheard of—well, perhaps!" he said. "But a commission I'd carry out with the best will in the world if I had the least assurance Addison would marry the girl! As he certainly won't, I must beg Miss Chenevix to hold me excused. And now I'm off. I have wasted far too much time here already."

He walked out of the room with this unceremonious leavetaking, and a few moments later they heard the front door close behind him.

Kitty burst into violent tears again. "I *will* go to Welwyn—I will, I *will*!" she declared, at which moment the knocker sounded below.

"Good God!" said Lady Constance, looking at Kitty with marked disfavour. "I daresay I had best tell Harbage we are at home to no one for the rest of the day!"

But before she could convey these instructions to him, rapid footsteps were heard upon the stairs, and the next moment Captain Harries walked into the room.

CHAPTER 17

Rossiter, driving his own phaeton and greys and sparing no effort to make the best time to his destination, arrived at the White Hart in Welwyn little more than a quarter hour after the moment when Cressida, with the green-coated man's hand firmly clamped over her mouth, had been driven away from it in the chaise. He at once alighted and, being approached by the landlord, who had come out to greet personally the owner of such a dashing and expensive equipage, enquired of him whether a young lady, travelling alone in a chaise, had shortly before arrived at his hostelry.

The landlord looked blank. A young lady? No, indeed, he had welcomed no young lady, travelling alone or otherwise, at his inn that day.

"Deuce take it, man, she must have arrived here!" Rossiter said impatiently. "I have certainly not passed her on the road; I made sure of that!"

The landlord, scenting romance, said sympathetically that he was very sorry, but there was indeed no young lady staying at his inn.

"And no gentleman named Addison, either, I daresay!" said Rossiter irritably.

He gave a terse description of the man he was seeking, which appeared to enlighten the landlord considerably, for he said at its conclusion, "Why, sir, *that's* the
Honourable Mr. Drew Addison you're speaking of, and I
know him well; he has a hunting-box not half a dozen
miles from here. But he hasn't been next or nigh my inn
today; I'll take my Bible oath on that!"

Rossiter, who was by this time beginning to have a
very distinct idea how the land lay, said he would have a
word with the ostlers who were then on duty and pro-
ceeded to do so; and at the end of five minutes, with the
aid of some intelligent questions and several silver coins,
had elicited the information that a chaise, in which one
of the ostlers had glimpsed a young lady in a close
bonnet, had indeed come into the yard a short time
before, with its postillions in a tearing hurry for a
change, and had departed as soon as this had been
accomplished, having taken up in the interval a large
man in a green coat who had been hanging around the
yard for an hour or more, as if awaiting its arrival.

A few further questions brought him explicit direc-
tions as to the location of Addison's hunting-box, and
within minutes he was on his way there through the
long, gathering midsummer twilight, his anxiety by this
time far predominating over the mingled euphoria and
exasperation that had carried him to Welwyn.

The house, almost invisible behind its dark screen
of trees, showed little sign of occupancy as his phaeton
rolled swiftly up the drive and came to a halt before the
front door. As he leaped down, however, and quickly
tethered the horses, the door opened and he saw framed
on the threshold a large man in a green coat, who enquired in a suspicious tone what his business was.

"Tell Mr. Addison," said Rossiter tersely, "that he
has a visitor," and, coming up the steps, he attempted to
enter the house.

The large man in the green coat solidly barred his way.

"Now, just a minute, guv'nor—" the large man began, and was on the instant thrust aside by a powerful shoulder.

Rossiter walked into the hall, only to find himself confronting another villainous-looking rascal, almost as large and intimidating as the first.

"Kindly inform Mr. Addison that he has a visitor," Rossiter repeated, with a negligent air that took both the men completely off guard, for as the second villain waited complacently for the first to come up behind this unexpected and unwanted caller and seize him, the caller himself suddenly turned and, with a single stunning blow, sent the green-coated man staggering back against the wall, his hands grasping at empty air.

The second villain, recovering from his surprise at this unanticipated manoeuvre, at once bored in upon Rossiter, only to find himself the recipient of an equally punishing blow that sent him crashing into a pier table that stood beside him, overturning it with considerable noise.

The sound and confusion of these proceedings naturally penetrated into the dining room where Cressida, still racking her brains for some means to extricate herself from the extremely unpleasant situation into which she had fallen, sat at the table with Addison, distastefully eating cold chicken and fruit as slowly as possible in order to prolong to its utmost length the period before Addison might begin pressing far more unwelcome attentions upon her. She had had little hope of rescue from any source beyond her own wits, for she was aware that even if Lady Constance, upon consideration, had taken sufficient alarm over the matter to send someone after her, he, or they, would have no idea where to find her; and her heart leapt up with the joy of unanticipated hope as the melee continued in the hall outside.

She had glanced at Addison as it had begun, and had noted the startled frown upon his face which indicated that his surprise was quite as great as her own. Now she saw him rise from his chair, his eyes going quickly about the room, apparently in search of some weapon, for he strode over at once to the fireplace and took down one of the pair of duelling rapiers that hung crossed over it.

The next moment the door to the hall had opened, and Rossiter, in a state of slight dishevelment, and with a trickle of blood coming from a cut beside one eye, came rapidly into the room. His eyes briefly raked the scene before him—Addison standing beside the fireplace with the rapier in his hand, Cressida seated at the table, her hand, still holding a fork carrying a morsel of chicken, suspended in midair as it had halted at the sound of the altercation beyond the door. Then, as a rush of footsteps sounded in the hall, he turned swiftly, closed and locked the door behind him, and dropped the key into his pocket.

"And now," he said scathingly, ignoring the heavy pounding that immediately began upon the door behind him, "now, if you please, Addison, I'll have the reason why, since you are apparently merely enjoying an agreeable supper tête-à-tête with Miss Calverton, you find it necessary to employ a pair of hired bravos to prevent your being interrupted—"

Cressida jumped up from the table, preventing herself with difficulty from flinging her arms about Rossiter's neck in her joy at seeing him walk into the room.

"But it *isn't* an agreeable supper!" she said earnestly. "He made me stay, with those two horrid men outside the door, just as he had one of them practically kidnap me in Welwyn and bring me here—" She broke off, suddenly becoming aware of the tense, wary, furious faces of the two men and the rapier gleaming in Addison's hand. "Oh, Dev, *do* let us go at once!" she said. "*Do* take me back to London! I've been such a fool—!"

"That—yes!" Rossiter said, in the same scathing tone in which he had previously spoken; but his eyes did not leave Addison's face. "It in no way excuses Mr. Addison's part in this affair, however—"

"Would you like satisfaction, Rossiter?—is that it?" Addison asked silkily.

"To call you out? I should like it very much!" Rossiter said grimly. "But not over this matter!"

"Yes—you *would* cut a rather poor figure, wouldn't you?" Addison said tauntingly. "The jilted lover is never an admired part, I believe, and duels attract such a disagreeable amount of notoriety these days." The pounding on the door continued unabated. "Good God, what noisy fellows!" he drawled. "I am afraid they may have used you a bit roughly in their zeal to protect my privacy. That cut upon your face—"

"—will not prevent me from serving you some of the same fare I gave them," Rossiter said, advancing purposefully upon him. "One against one this time, Addison—fairer odds, don't you think?"

He was within a few feet of Addison when the rapier flashed out suddenly, the point touching the cloth of his coat and holding him pinned there.

"Oh, no, my dear fellow—not so fast!" Addison said, with an unpleasant smile. "I have no taste, I fear, for fisticuffs, and you, I understand from the habitués of Gentleman Jackson's Boxing Saloon, are quite a nonpareil at that sort of thing. Now if you were as familiar at Angelo's" (naming the establishment where a famous fencing-master taught his art) "I might gratify your desire to match skills with me—"

Rossiter, without a change of countenance, stepped back a pace, disengaging himself from the rapier's point, and, moving to the fireplace, took down the remaining rapier.

"Dev—*no!*" cried Cressida, feeling suddenly quite sick with a horrid kind of alarm, for she was well aware that Addison was held to be one of the best swordsmen in a London which had at present little interest in this art, affairs of honour now being settled exclusively with pistols, so that Manton's Shooting Gallery was the place where gentlemen practised their more lethal skills. She sprang to Rossiter's side and laid her hand urgently upon his arm. "You mustn't!" she said. "Kitty and I—we've *both* been fools; but couldn't you leave it at that and come away?"

Rossiter glanced down at her impatiently. "Don't compound your folly by acting the fool a second time!" he commanded curtly. "I shan't kill him; you may be assured of that!"

"No, I think not!" said Addison, taking off his coat and pulling off his boots in such a coolly efficient way that Cressida's fears were instantly intensified.

She had been brought up on romantic novels, her great-aunt Estella having been unexpectedly addicted to this type of reading and having a large library of such works, but she had never been the kind of girl to enjoy imagining herself looking on in a candlelit room while two men fought with rapiers, if not precisely over her, at least over their pent-up wrath and dislike of each other because of a horrid little drama in which she had certainly played her part; and she suddenly felt so furious with both of them for putting her in a position where, if something happened to either of them, she would have to feel responsible for it, that if she had been able to, she would simply have walked out of the room and washed her hands of the whole affair.

But the door was locked and the key in Rossiter's pocket, so she had to content herself with closing her eyes very tightly together as the two men hastily pushed the heavy table and chairs out of their way and she heard the first harsh clash of steel upon steel.

She then remembered a three-volume novel in her great-aunt's library, that had contained an episode in which the heroine had rushed between the combatants in a duel, thus effectually putting a halt to it but receiving in the process a mortal wound herself, from which she had subsequently succumbed in an affecting death scene; but, being far too sensible not to realise that any interruption of the combatants' concentration upon their work was just as likely to result in a mortal wound to one of them as to herself, she put this self-sacrificial idea aside. Presently, unable to bear any longer the suspense of hearing only the scuffle of stockinged feet upon the floor, the quick, panting breathing of the two men, and the ring of steel on steel, without having the least notion of how the battle was going, she opened her eyes again.

There was a slit, she immediately noted, in Rossiter's left sleeve, from which a red stain was slowly spreading, but he himself seemed quite unaware of this. It was Addison, she saw, who was pushing the attack, displaying the brilliant foil-work that had made him one of Angelo's favourite pupils; but, try as he might, he was having no success in penetrating Rossiter's guard. Rossiter's own style was serviceable, stubborn, and of an iron endurance; and she realised after a time the strategy that lay behind it—to anticipate Addison's every move, to hold him off until he began to tire and, in a moment of fatigue or lost concentration, left himself open to Rossiter's own attack.

The pounding upon the door, she was aware, had ceased now; the two rogues, evidently wanting no part of the deadly battle they could hear going forward on its other side, had apparently taken themselves off. She thought, in desperation, of overturning the candelabrum upon the table, which was the room's only illumination, since the curtains had been drawn against the dusk outside; but in this case, too, she could not be certain that in the confusion of the moment in which she did so a fatal hit might not be made. She saw hopefully that, in spite of the fact that it was Rossiter's shirt that bore that spreading stain, it was Addison who was now obviously tiring; he was breathing in short, harsh gasps, and the speed and daring of his attack had lessened. Rossiter's own face was grim, wary, and implacable, as he parried that attack with a wrist and arm that seemed as flexible and tireless as the steel with which he fought.

And then, suddenly, his rapier flashed in a lightning lunge in high carte; a long, reddening slash appeared in Addison's right sleeve near the shoulder; and the blades disengaged. Addison's dropped to the floor with a clatter as he stood, gasping, his face as white as his shirt, clutching his sword arm in his left hand.

"Enough?" panted Rossiter, his face still grim and unforgiving. He strode forward quickly, dropping his own rapier, and, seizing Addison's arm, ripped the sleeve up quickly and examined the wound. "I told you I shouldn't kill you," he said then coolly, drawing his handkerchief from his pocket and binding it over the wound. "I admire your skill, by the way—but you lack staying power. We always found it so with the French—"

"Damn you, don't patronise me!" said Addison thickly. He sank down into a chair, his face colourless. "Can't stand the sight of blood—never could," he said, shuddering. "Give—brandy—"

"Your own blood, you mean," Rossiter said unsympathetically. "The sight of mine didn't appear to trouble you particularly."

He strode over to the sideboard, poured brandy from a decanter into a glass, and brought it over to his vanquished foe. At the same moment Cressida, who was in a state of such relief over Addison's defeat, anxiety concerning the wound that Rossiter had himself received, and fury with both of them for having frightened her almost out of her wits with their obstinate male insistence upon settling their differences at sword's point, that she had not yet recovered herself sufficiently to say a word, became aware of a renewed disturbance of some sort in the hall outside the locked door. Apprehension that Addison's disreputable henchmen had returned sent her eyes flying to Rossiter's. He glanced up.

"What the devil—!" he exclaimed. "Women's voices? Is that Lady Con?"

He walked over to the door, took the key from his pocket, unlocked it, and flung it open.

The next moment Lady Constance and Kitty, both talking at once, and followed by Captain Harries, who appeared to be attempting to restrain them, tumbled pell-mell into the room.

C H A P T E R 18

All three of the newcomers checked in astonishment at the tableau presented to them as they entered the room —the disarranged furniture, the rapiers lying discarded upon the floor, and Addison, very pale, seated beside the table with a glass of brandy in his shaking left hand and his right arm bound with a blood-soaked handkerchief, while Rossiter, also displaying the stains of combat, and Cressida, most unwontedly discomposed, stood staring at them in disbelief.

It was Lady Constance who first, majestically, gave voice to her own thoughts.

"You see," she said to Captain Harries, as if putting a definite end to an argument that had been going on between them for some time, "I was *quite* right to come with you. I had a premonition I should be needed, and it was far more agreeable than remaining at home, with Kitty having the vapours because you would not agree to take *her*. Cressy, my dear," she went on, stepping firmly into the room, "I do not know *what* has been happening here, but I can see that it has all been very distressing for you. In *my* day," she said, directing a disapproving glance at Rossiter, "gentlemen did not settle their disagreements in the presence of ladies."

"In *your* day," Rossiter retorted, with some heat and a disapproving glance of his own towards Cressida, "ladies did not thrust themselves into affairs that did not concern them."

But Kitty, who obviously found this academic discussion of the proprieties quite beside the point, here drew everyone's attention upon herself by flying across the room to Addison's side and dropping to her knees beside his chair.

"You are hurt!" she exclaimed rather redundantly, as he was already quite aware of the fact, as was everyone else in the room.

Addison made a gesture of distaste, which—as the glass of brandy was still in his hand—had the unlucky effect of splashing some of its contents upon her frock. As she recoiled, he said savagely, "My apologies, ma'am!—though perhaps, more correctly, you should be offering me yours, since it is through your curst poor management that I find myself in this case! Perhaps on the next occasion you plan to elope you will manage to keep the matter to yourself, instead of allowing it to become the property of meddling outsiders!"

"But I *didn't*—!" Kitty began, looking shocked at the violence of this attack from the ordinarily urbane Addison. "Indeed, it was not my fault, and I am quite ready to m-marry you tomorrow, no matter what Lady Constance may say—"

Addison gave a disagreeable laugh. "Charming of you—but, as your very astute guardians have long since guessed, marriage was never in the picture, my dear," he said.

Kitty looked at him incredulously. "But you *can't* mean—!" she faltered.

"On the contrary," said Lady Constance briskly, "it

is exactly what he has meant all along, you foolish, foolish girl. But now, if you please," she when on, advancing upon Addison as Kitty, bursting into tears, jumped up and would have run from the room if she had not been restrained by Captain Harries, against whose broad shoulder she was able to sob out her disappointment and disillusionment very comfortably, "*now*, Addison, I shall have a look at your wound. You are looking very green, and that horrid, clumsy bandage you are wearing is obviously not stopping the bleeding."

As the rest of the company gazed respectfully, she untied the rough bandage Rossiter had made from his handkerchief and clicked her tongue disapprovingly over the deep wound in the flesh of the upper arm that was thus revealed.

"You will no doubt," she pronounced judicially, "be in a high fever by morning; it is bed for you at once, sir. Are there any servants in the house?"

"None," articulated Addison with some difficulty, for he was looking decidedly faint at the renewed sight of the wound.

"Very well, then; Captain Rossiter and Captain Harries will help you upstairs to your bedchamber," Lady Constance said decisively, as she replaced the bandage.

Cressida, recovering her voice for the first time, said indignantly that Rossiter was wounded, too.

"A mere scratch, it would seem," declared Lady Constance, dismissing the unimpressive stain upon Rossiter's shirt-sleeve with a glance. "You may, however, bathe it and put some Basilicum Powder on it, if there is any to be found in the house, as soon as he has helped Addison to bed."

She gestured imperatively to Captain Harries, who, obediently putting the weeping Kitty aside, came over and, with Rossiter's aid, assisted Addison to his feet.

Addison stumbled off between them, with Lady Constance leading the way up the stairs and Cressida and Kitty following rather uncertainly behind.

In a bedchamber at the head of the stairs candle-light glowed softly over a scene of sybaritic luxury that reminded Cressida forcibly of some of the more colourful descriptions of Eastern seraglios in Lord Byron's much admired poems. There were silken hangings and tasselled cushions, even a purple velvet robe flung with ostentatious carelessness across the bed; and Cressida, regarding this evidence of a totally unexpected romanticism in the astringent Addison, suddenly found herself on the verge of giving way to a fit of the giggles, like a schoolgirl.

No doubt, she told herself severely, it was the disordered state of her nerves that was causing this unseemly reaction to the sight of the scene prepared for Kitty's—and then, by default, her own—seduction; but then her eyes caught Rossiter's; she saw her own amusement mirrored in his; and her heart suddenly lightened in a most extraordinary fashion, as if all the terrors of the past hour had melted away like a summer morning mist.

Lady Constance, meanwhile, after glancing about the room with obvious distaste, ordered Rossiter and Harries to help Addison to bed, and herself departed, with Cressida and Kitty in tow, in search of bandages and medicaments. Having ruthlessly dismembered a fine linen sheet for the former purpose and resigned herself to nothing more restorative than hartshorn and Basilicum Powder for the latter, she returned to her patient, who was by this time propped up on the pillows in his gorgeous bed, looking more ghastly than ever.

"We shall have to fetch a surgeon to him, of course," she said, briskly taking command once more. "Captain Harries, will you be good enough to drive back to Welwyn at once and fetch the local man? Captain Rossiter will remain here and have his own wound—which I apprehend is not at all serious and therefore does not require *my* attention—tended to by you, my dear Cressy. Kitty, you will remain here with me. I shall require your assistance in dealing with Mr. Addison."

Kitty, tear-stained and resentful, looked as if she would much rather have gone with Captain Harries, who obviously appeared to her as her only present anchor in the storm of events that had wrecked all her hopes; but Lady Constance, in the spirit of command that had fallen upon her, was plainly going to brook no opposition, so Kitty remained where she was. Captain Harries, equally obedient, went off down the stairs, and Cressida, commandeering a supply of Basilicum Powder and some strips of linen, led a still amused Rossiter across the hall to a second bedchamber.

"Is she always like this?" he demanded, as he sat down in a chair beside the washstand and watched her pouring water from the pitcher into the bowl. "Good God, I hadn't suspected she could be such a martinet!"

"Nor had I," Cressida confessed, for some reason avoiding his eyes out of a sudden, inexplicable feeling of violent shyness. "I expect she is—what one might call, *rising to the occasion*. Just as *you* did," she added in a much lower voice, industriously bending all her attention to the task of wetting a cloth with which to bathe his wound, "when you came to my rescue just now. I—I have been too much overset to thank you properly—"

There was no response. She was obliged to look up, and found that he was regarding her with a most extraordinary expression, which appeared to be compounded partly of amusement and partly of something far more unfathomable and disturbing, in his dark eyes.

"Gratitude—from *you*, Cressy?" he quizzed her. "Unnecessary, I should think! Is it possible that you hadn't already formulated some brilliant scheme of your own for outwitting Addison and making your escape before I came upon the scene?"

Cressida, who had been about to roll up the torn sleeve of his shirt in order to lay bare his wound, halted in the act of doing so and picked up the bowl instead, as if it offered her some sort of protection from that disturbing expression in his eyes.

"Well," she admitted, "I *was* considering throwing the contents of the pepper-pot into his eyes and escaping through the window while he was temporarily blinded. But I wasn't *quite* sure I could run faster than those two horrid men—"

She paused indignantly, as Rossiter broke into a shout of laughter.

"Oh, Cressy, my darling," he gasped, when he could speak again, "I'll back you against a score of Addisons any day in the week! I was fit to murder him when I came in and saw what he had in mind; in fact, I was fit to murder you, too, for getting yourself into a scrape like that! But I ought to have known—"

He broke off, seeing that she was observing him with a very odd expression upon her own face, rather, he told her later, as if she had seen something explode and was waiting to see if it would do it again.

"Oh! What did you say?" she enquired faintly, after a moment. "You called me 'my darling'—but you are engaged to Kitty—"

"I am not, at the present moment, engaged to Miss Chenevix or to anyone else," Rossiter corrected her firmly. "But I am quite willing to be engaged to *you*, if given even half a chance." He rose abruptly, and Cressida found herself enveloped in an exceedingly urgent embrace that appeared to be quite unconscious of the drawbacks presented by bloodstains, precariously held basins filled with water, and the rather improper fact that they were alone together in another man's bedchamber. Cressida hastily set the bowl down, which was the only one of the drawbacks she herself was aware of at the moment, thus allowing the embrace to tighten even more ruthlessly about her. "I am afraid," Rossiter's voice said over her head, "that Lady Con has betrayed you, Cressy. She told me—I can only hope correctly—that you were in love with me—"

"Well, I *am*," said Cressida, developing a great interest in the top button of his shirt, so that it was obviously quite impossible for her to look up into his face. "Oh, Dev, I've *always* been—only I thought, all these years, that you wanted me to break off our engagement because you had had second thoughts about marrying a girl with no fortune—" She looked up at him, overcome by sudden indignation. "Well, how was I to imagine that you were only being noble?" she demanded. "You, of all men—"

"And that," said Rossiter reflectively, "puts me nicely in my place, and is my just reward, no doubt, for trying for once in my life to act the *preux chevalier*. But how the devil was I to carry you off to follow the drum on a marching officer's pay when you stood to gain a fortune by the simple fact of my walking out of your life?"

"You might have left the decision to *me*," Cressida said, still as indignant as it was possible for her to be with his arms about her and her breast pressed so closely to his that she could feel the strong beating of his heart. "If you were so idiotish as to believe a fortune could make me happy—well, it hasn't! I *tried* to love other people, but I never could—"

"Which is as good an excuse as any, I suppose, for the sort of behaviour that gave *me* every right to believe you had turned into the most heartless flirt in London!" Rossiter said, his dark eyes laughing down at her. "Oh, Cressy, Cressy, what the *devil* of a coil you have put us both through, practically pitchforking me into the arms of that wretched girl, jilting poor Langmere—"

"It was not all *my* fault!" Cressida protested, attempting, rather vainly, to speak with some hauteur. "You should have come back sooner! After all, Great-aunt Estella has been dead for years."

"As a matter of fact, I did come back," Rossiter said, "having the poorest opinion of myself as a fellow who had waited only for you to take possession of your fortune before renewing my suit—but then I was still top-over-tail in love, you see, and nobility was wearing rather thin by that time! Only I found you had meanwhile gotten yourself engaged to young Mennin, so it seemed there was nothing for me to do but take myself off again—"

"But I didn't *know* then that you were in love with me," she protested.

"Nor I that you still cared a button for me," said Rossiter, and looked down at her with such doubt suddenly in his dark face that she felt her heart turn over with love. "It's true, isn't it?" he asked. "You *do* care? I've never really dared to hope—not after I walked into Mayr's office that morning and you looked at me as if I were something you'd turned up under a rock in the garden—"

"I was *odious*," Cressida said violently. "I wonder you ever wanted to *see* me again after that! *I* shouldn't have, if I had been you."

But Rossiter declared that not only had he wished then, and always would, to see her again and again and again, but that it was his present intention never to let her out of his sight, no matter how many other people she got engaged to; at which point matters suddenly arrived at such a pass that they were whirled backward in time to become in some mysterious fashion a much younger Captain Deverell Rossiter and a shy and eager Cressy Calverton tasting her first experience of love in the very proper garden of her great-aunt Estella's Cheltenham villa.

Lady Constance, entering the room without warning, found the fashionable Miss Calverton kissing and being kissed by her tall Captain in a manner that would have astonished the London *ton*, accustomed as they were to considering her a young lady who, however dashing, never lost her elegant composure.

"This is all very well, Cressy dear," she said, observing with disapproval the unsullied water in the bowl upon the washstand and Rossiter's unbandaged condition, "and I am very happy to see that you and Captain Rossiter have made up your differences, since it is quite beyond the bounds of reason to expect him to marry Kitty now; but this is *not* what I sent you here to do."

She picked up the strip of linen that Cressida had wetted in the bowl and, advancing ruthlessly upon Rossiter, thus obliging him to relinquish his hold upon Cressida, laid bare his injured arm and advised him, in a tone that brooked no opposition, to seat himself while she attended to it. Cressida, in a daze of happiness, looked somewhat rebellious at having the task of ministering to her beloved thus reft from her, but, realising that in her present state she would be far less competent than Lady Constance to do what needed to be done, she contented herself with standing beside him and holding his free hand except when Lady Constance, having finished with his arm, demanded that place for herself so that she could bathe the cut upon his face and put court-plaster upon it.

"I can't think what you can have been doing to get yourself into such a condition!" she said severely. "Have you been in an accident, in addition to fighting with swords with Addison?—*quite* an outmoded method of duelling, but one which I, personally, find far more romantic than pistols, reminding me as it does of my younger days."

Here she looked so sibylline that Cressida and Rossiter regarded her with respectful awe, envisioning dozens of the bewigged, gorgeously satin-coated dandies of an earlier day destroying one another for her favours.

Cressida said proudly that Rossiter had been obliged to overpower two enormous ruffians before he had been able to proceed to rescue her from Addison.

"How very disagreeable!" Lady Constance said placidly. "Where can they have taken themsclves off to, I wonder? There is literally no one but ourselves in the house, so that I am very much afraid we shall have to remain here to look after that wretched Addison until someone else can be found to do it. However, I daresay it is all for the best in the end, for it will certainly be quite dark by the time Captian Harries returns with the surgeon, and I have not the least desire to drive all the way back to Welwyn tonight."

Cressida, coming out of the new bliss of her happiness, pointed out practically that none of them had dined, and, as there were no servants in the house, it appeared likely that they would be obliged to forage for themselves, and perhaps without a great deal of success.

"Nonsense!" said Lady Constance briskly. "It appeared to me that there was a very acceptable supper laid in the dining room when we came in, and if there is not a sufficiency for everyone, I am sure *something* will be found in the kitchen. I daresay the gentlemen will be happy to dine upon bread and cheese, as Addison, I understand, is an excellent judge of wine and there must certainly be a bottle of something fit to drink in the house."

Rossiter, who was feeling a little drunk with happiness at the moment without benefit of wine, excellent or otherwise, said that for his part he could live on love, though he would not say no to bread and cheese, but that in his opinion they made a very odd sort of house-party, and the surgeon, finding his patient suffering from a sword wound, might very well insist on taking the matter before a magistrate.

"Oh, no!" said Lady Constance superbly. "Not at all, my dear man! I shall tell him that, as there are no servants in the house, Addison was obliged to help me cut up a chicken for our supper and wounded himself quite by accident."

Rossiter gave a shout of laughter, and Cressida, though enthralled by the mental picture of the elegant Addison dismembering a fowl, protested, "But he won't believe you!"

"Of course he won't. But he won't be able to *prove* that it wasn't so," said Lady Constance triumphantly, "which is what is always so useful about lies. I mean, it is other people who have to prove they aren't true. And," she added, her eyes kindling ominously, "if Addison says a *word* to the contrary, he knows very well what sort of tales will shortly be making the rounds about *him*. But he won't. He has told me that he intends to take my advice and go abroad for an indefinite stay—which I would say is a *far* better fate than he deserves, except that I have never seen you look so happy, my dear Cressy, which is all *his* doing if one really examines the matter. And then I daresay I shall be able to get Kitty off, too, in the end. Captain Harries seems *quite* taken with her, and I am sure this experience will suffice to lower her crest a little and cause her to see the value of True Worth in a man, rather than looking for nothing but Fortune. Which reminds me," she added complacently, "that I may have neglected to tell you previously that Sir Octavius Mayr and I have decided to be married in the autumn."

Cressida stared at her, quite staggered by this totally unexpected bombshell.

"You and Octavius—!" she exclaimed. "But you can't—! I mean, you've only just met him!"

"Yes, my dear, but you see he has such a lovely house and such beautiful things in it, and it does become so very tiresome, perpetually being an impecunious widow," Lady Constance said, picking up the court-plaster and the Basilicum Powder and preparing to return to her other patient. "You have always told me that he is the wisest man you know, and it seems you were quite right. He made up his mind at first sight, he told me, that I am exactly the chatelaine his house—or I should say his house, for he tells me he has a very agreeable place in Kent—require. My Plantagenet blood, you see: when one is a collector, it seems, one wishes for only the finest. So he broached the matter to me on the spot, at his dinner-party—I *do* adore a man of decision, who sweeps one quite off one's feet!—and then we met very privately at my solicitor's this morning and set all the arrangements in train. I may add that the settlements he is making upon me are *most* generous."

And she walked out of the room, leaving Rossiter and Cressida to stare at each other in an astonished silence.

"No, I *can't* believe it!" Cressida said after a moment. "Octavius and Lady Con! Of course he *has* always had a secret ambition to ally himself with Royalty—I believe so many Royal Houses are indebted to him for financial aid that he rather thinks he is deserving of the distinction—and Lady Con really *has* Plantagenet blood. But it has always raised her bristles, you know, when I have merely mentioned his name!"

"Ah, but *that* was before he had proposed marriage to her," Rossiter reminded her, with laughter in his eyes. "I have noticed that that makes a great difference to most females, particularly if one has a considerable fortune to offer along with one's hand and heart. In our own case, thank God, it seems unlikely that either of us is marrying the other for his or her fortune, unless one of us is inordinately greedy or you have decided that it is worth taking me so you may get Calverton Place into your hands."

"Wretch!" said Cressida, who had found that, in the

absence of a convenient sofa or tête-à-tête she could share with her love, a footstool drawn up beside the chair in which Lady Constance had obliged him to sit offered a highly satisfactory substitute, enabling his arm to go about her in a very agreeable and comfortable way. "I still can't think why you wished to have it, except to spite me—but I have decided to forgive you, since I must confess that the only reason *I* wished to have it was to spite *you*. And it is very nice, I daresay, that we are both so rich now that neither of us needs to marry for money." she went on, "but I *do* think you should have known, my darling, that I would *far* rather have married you years ago and not have had Great-aunt Estella's fortune."

"I know it now," said Rossiter, and was about to demonstrate how earth-shakingly important he found that knowledge when Lady Constance came back into the room and said that, since Addison was as comfortable as she could make him, she and Kitty were going downstairs to see what could be done about supper, and would they care to come with them?

"No!" said Cressida and Rossiter in one breath; upon which Lady Constance looked at them indulgently.

"Very well; five minutes, then," she conceded. "We shall need you to open the wine, Captain Rossiter, if any is to be found. And remember that you will have all the rest of your lives together."

Whereupon she went away, looking more sibylline than ever.

"The rest of our lives!" Cressida said, sighing happily. "What a lovely thought!"

"Yes, but only five minutes now, remember," Rossiter reminded her, and, unwilling to lose any of that precious time, he forthwith drew her to him and kissed her.